You'll be howling for more
My Brother the Werewolf!

Cry Wolf!

Puppy Love!

Howl-oween – coming soon!

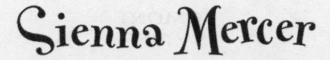

Sienna Mercer

MY BROTHER THE WEREWOLF

PUPPY LOVE!

EGMONT

EGMONT

We bring stories to life

With special thanks to Stephanie Burgis

My Brother the Werewolf: Puppy Love! first published in Great Britain 2013
by Egmont UK Limited
The Yellow Building, 1 Nicholas Road, London W11 4AN

Copyright © Working Partners Ltd 2013
Created by Working Partners Limited, London WC1X 9HH

ISBN 978 1 4052 6439 6

1 3 5 7 9 10 8 6 4 2

A CIP catalogue record for this title is available from the British Library

Typeset by Avon DataSet Ltd, Bidford on Avon, Warwickshire
Printed and bound in Great Britain by the CPI Group

53025/1

MIX
Paper
FSC FSC® C018306

EGMONT LUCKY COIN

Our story began over a century ago, when seventeen-year-old
Egmont Harald Petersen found a coin in the street.

He was on his way to buy a flyswatter, a small hand-operated
printing machine that he then set up in his tiny apartment.

The coin brought him such good luck that today Egmont has
offices in over 30 countries around the world. And that lucky
coin is still kept at the company's head offices in Denmark.

For Patrick and Jamie, with love

Chapter One

*D*on't panic, Justin Packer ordered himself. *This is not a* date!

Yes, he was sharing a booth at the Meat & Greet with Riley Carter. Yes, she was the girl he'd been crushing on for nearly a year. And no, there wasn't anybody else sitting at the table with them. But that didn't make this an *official* date . . .

Or, did it?

Friends have meals together all the time, he told himself. *Eating is* totally *essential.*

Someday soon, he *would* ask Riley out. But before he'd be ready to ask Riley on a real date, he had to treat it like a football game. He had to *prepare* – have a game plan. He had to learn how to keep his cool around her even when she was smiling at him the way she was now, with her intense, focused eyes seeming to shine through the long strands of blonde hair that were falling chaotically over her face. He'd have to figure out how to be . . . *suave*.

Yeah, he'd be totally suave when he eventually did ask her out on a *real* date. For now, they would stay friends. There was no pressure in friendship.

Relaxing, Justin reached for his hamburger – then froze with it part-way to his mouth as he saw Riley tucking the rebellious locks of hair behind her ears. She looked very pretty.

Wait a minute. Is she trying *to look good? For me?*

His stomach clenched. *What if we actually* are *on a date, and I didn't even realise? Is she judging my dating skills? I haven't* prepared *for this – I don't have a game plan! I can't be judged when it's not a date. And it's not. It really, truly is —*

'Notadate!' he blurted through his hamburger.

Then he cringed as he realised that he'd said it out loud.

'Justin?' Riley frowned at him across the table. 'Are you choking?'

'Me?' Justin swallowed hard. 'No! Everything's cool. Totally cool. Totally, absolutely, definitely . . .' As her eyebrows rose, he felt his cheeks heat up. He set down the hamburger. 'I mean, it's just . . . cool, isn't it, that we can hang out like this . . . as friends?'

Riley's hand fell away from her hair, her gaze dropping to the table. 'Um, I guess. If that's what you think.'

Justin knew that if this conversation was a football, he had carried it into a wall of defenders, and would now have to scramble to find another route. He needed something else to talk about.

'Look at Daniel and Debi!' he said, pointing across the diner. 'They're not on a date, are they? They're just hanging out. Just like we are . . .'

Although . . . Justin's eyes narrowed as he looked across at his twin, who was wearing his usual scruffy black clothing and sitting across a table from Riley's friend Debi. With his brooding rock-musician style, Daniel might look like the polar opposite of perky cheerleader Debi, but the two of them weren't just sharing a meal. They'd gone to see that new Jackson Caulfield movie, *The Groves*, earlier, too.

I've scrambled into another tackle, he thought. *Those two are* definitely *on a date, which means that Riley must think we are, too!*

'Um, Justin?' Riley's voice broke into his panic. 'You seem a little nervous.'

'Me? Nervous? No way!' Justin grabbed the

last of his hamburger and took a huge bite. 'I don't get nervous,' he said, through his mouthful. Then he looked down at his empty plate, and almost choked again.

'Oh,' said Riley. 'I thought it was nerves making you gobble your food like a ravenous wolf.'

Wolf!

If only, Justin thought, and sighed. *That would make my life so much easier!* As the only non-werewolf playing Offense on Pine Wood Junior High's football team, he had to do everything he could to bulk up his ordinary human body and make himself stronger. But he couldn't explain that to Riley. That would be the exact opposite of guarding the secret of werewolves' existence, which *no one* was supposed to know. The only reason Justin knew was because his dad was a werewolf – and until a month ago, he'd always expected to become one, too.

But the 'Lupine gene' in the family had scrambled away from Justin, towards his twin brother.

'I'm just trying to pile on the calories,' he mumbled. 'For the Homecoming Game next week.'

Luckily, the mention of Homecoming had been enough to spark off Riley's famous Organisational Mode. She sat bolt upright, her eyes gleaming with excitement. 'Can you believe it's only a week away now? There is so much left to do! I've been planning and planning, but –'

'You, planning? *Never.*' Justin shook his head at her, grinning. 'You know, there's going to be some epic homework this year. Why don't you go easy on yourself, and take the year off from being Pine Wood's Chief Organiser?'

Riley just looked at him. Then they both burst into laughter.

Date or no date, Justin had known Riley since kindergarten, and knew that the day that she *didn't* organise anything and everything in her path would be the day that every big, tough werewolf on the football team requested lettuce and cucumber sandwiches for their pre-game meal.

'Let me tell you what I've been thinking . . .' Riley began.

A sudden tug at Justin's wrist made him jump. When he glanced down, he blinked twice, just to make sure he was really seeing what he thought he saw.

Daniel?

Justin's twin was crouched beside his booth, out of sight of Riley, who was busy pulling out two different clipboards from her shoulder bag. When Justin opened his mouth to speak, Daniel shook his head violently and held one finger to his mouth. Then he pointed at the door with a gesture that clearly meant: *Outside. Now!*

Justin nodded. Still disbelieving, he watched Daniel stoop-walk away.

His not-a-date must be going even worse than my not-a-date.

Luckily, Riley didn't seem to have noticed any of the byplay. All of her focus was centred on the points she was ticking off her first three-page-long list.

'. . . and of course, the Homecoming Dance has to be absolutely *perfect*, so –'

'Wait, what?' Justin blinked. 'The *Dance*? I thought you were putting in to organise stuff for the Homecoming *game*!'

'Have you forgotten who you're talking to?' Riley rolled her eyes at him. 'I'm volunteering for both, obviously.'

'Obviously.' Justin shook his head. 'I should have known.'

As their gazes met, Justin felt himself go dizzy for a moment. There was a light in her eyes that pulled him in, making him want to lean across the table towards her and . . .

Get a grip, cub! It was what Coach Johnston told the football players when they lost focus. Justin took a deep breath, shaking off the sudden urge to throw aside everything he'd planned and make it a real date after all.

He'd promised Daniel to meet him outside. His twin needed him! And he needed to keep himself on-target. *Remember that pre-date training?*

'I'll be right back,' he told Riley as he stood up. 'OK?'

'Oh. OK.' She settled back, her lips curving down in what looked like disappointment. By the time Justin had reached the door of the diner, though, he could see her bent over her Homecoming list again, totally absorbed.

He found Daniel hiding around the corner of the Meat & Greet, out of sight of the windows – in the doorway of a thrift store that seemed to specialise in dusty hardback books and too-colourful charm bracelets. 'What's going on?'

'Finally!' Daniel's eyes looked wild. 'You have to save me. Look!' He rolled up the long sleeve of his black shirt, emblazoned with the scrawled logo for his band, *In Sheep's Clothing*. Thick hair had sprouted all across his arms. A clear sign of panic in any teenage werewolf.

Justin winced in sympathy, forgetting his own problems. 'I guess Debi's been driving you *lupe*-y, huh?' Then he laughed at his own joke.

'Will you take this seriously?' Daniel glared at him, rolling his sleeve down. Then he rolled it back up again to itch at the back of one hand. 'I am in deep trouble! If I have to sit across from her for one more minute, hair's going to start sprouting on my hands and face, too.'

Justin could see Daniel's canine teeth growing as he flipped out. 'How are you ever going to have a real date with Debi if you turn into a wolf every time you're around her?'

'I'll find a way around it,' Daniel said. 'Somehow.' His shoulders slumped. 'I just need to have a few more practice dates, you know?'

Justin *did* know. 'So . . .' Justin raised his eyebrows. 'What are you planning to do today? Make an escape?'

'I'm not going to just ditch her,' Daniel said. 'That would be mean. My date will continue . . .' He looked at Justin, his face set with determination.

Justin's mouth dropped open as it dawned on him what Daniel was saying-without-saying. 'No way! It's *your* not-date, not mine.'

'It's just until she finishes her lunch,' Daniel

said. 'Do you really want me to be responsible for letting out the werewolf secret to the world?'

Justin groaned. 'You know I don't. But —'

'I've done it for you,' Daniel said. 'Remember your first football game?'

Daniel had saved Justin's butt by taking his place during the first game of the season. 'Fine,' he said. 'But we'll have to swap shirts. Riley might be distracted by all her planning, but even she'd notice if "I" came back wearing *In Sheep's Clothing* merchandise!'

Daniel hesitated. 'But . . . this is "limited edition".'

Justin stepped forward and started tugging at his brother's collar. 'Of course it is — you've only made *one*.'

By the time he sat down in Justin and Riley's booth, Daniel was already feeling better. His skin wasn't itching, his nails weren't growing, his ears hadn't changed shape and his teeth weren't tingling. He was totally, completely relaxed . . .

. . . or, at least, he *was* until Riley looked up from the list in her hands, biting her lip. 'Justin?'

Daniel said nothing.

Riley blinked at him. 'Justin?'

A voice in his head roared: *You're not 'Daniel' any more, doofus!*

'Yeah?' he blurted. 'I am Justin.'

Riley frowned, her eyes narrowing for just a moment, before she shook her head. 'Do you think your brother would freak if I suggested that our band audition to play at Homecoming?'

'What?!' Daniel felt his jaw drop. '*In Sheep's Clothing?*' He had started the band that summer, and Riley – preppy, upbeat Riley – had shocked

13

everyone when she won the audition to be their lead singer.

'Yeah,' she said. 'Unless we started another band as a side-project? I mean, that does *sound* like me, but I think I'd have remembered.'

Daniel shook his head in disbelief. 'You want us – I mean, *them* – to play at Homecoming? *Seriously?*'

She nodded. Daniel felt his head whirl with horror.

Be Justin! he ordered himself. *Be Justin!*

Justin would never yell *'No way!'* to that question. Justin probably wouldn't question anything that made Riley happy, even if what made Riley happy was volunteering the band to play at a barn dance.

Daniel tried to smile like Justin. *That shouldn't be hard*, he thought, *considering we have the exact same face.* Still, even he could hear the strain in his voice as he answered. 'You can always ask him,' he said. 'But I have to warn you, Daniel has some . . . *opinions* on mainstream school stuff like Homecoming.'

'Opinions, hmm?' Riley tapped her pen against her lips. 'Well, I'm sure I can talk him into it. I'll prepare some really good arguments.'

Daniel clamped his jaw shut to hold back the howl of protest that wanted to escape. Desperately, he looked down at Justin's plate for a distraction. It was empty.

Argh. He'd been so nervous with Debi, he hadn't had even a single bite of his own meal. He was starving! But if he ordered more food, that might make Riley think Justin was weird. Daniel couldn't let that happen.

It was only when Riley cleared her throat that he realised just how long he'd been staring at the empty plate. *Uh-oh.*

'Justin?' Riley shook her head, her eyebrows scrunched with worry. 'Are you *still* hungry?'

'Nope,' Daniel muttered. Then his stomach rumbled so loudly, he had to speak just to cover it up. 'I'm fine! Totally normal appetite. Really.'

'Ohh-kay,' Riley said. 'If you say so.'

'Totally.' Daniel forced a smile. *Distract! Distract!* 'So,' he said, pointing at the list in her hands. 'Do you have your eye on any committees in particular?'

Riley stared at him. 'I just *told* you five minutes ago – I'm applying for the Homecoming Game and Dance organisation jobs. Remember?'

'Oh!' Daniel winced. 'Right.'

Riley looked hurt. 'Weren't you listening?'

'Of course I was!' *Maybe I should have asked Justin to prep me before I took over for him.* 'But why don't you remind me what you've got planned so far?'

It was a fool-proof way to get Riley started. As

she launched into the mile-a-minute description of her plans, Daniel tuned out, leaning back against the wall of the booth.

Now let's see how Justin's me-impersonation is doing.

Opening up his senses, he tuned in his werewolf-sharp hearing to the voices coming out of Debi and Justin's booth.

Debi's voice was as sweet as always, but for some reason, it was starting to sound a little desperate. 'So, did you even *like* the movie?'

There was a long silence. Then Justin said, his tone as bleak as if he were at a funeral: '. . . Yeah.'

Yeah? Daniel winced. *Is that really all you can think of?*

Debi's voice was definitely sounding strained now. 'What about the movie theatre? I think the new screens are great, don't you?'

Another long silence felt like torture against Daniel's ears. Finally – *finally!* – he heard his

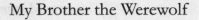

brother say, 'Well. They don't . . . really . . . *rock*, do you know what I mean?'

Daniel cringed and sank lower in his seat. *Nobody in the world would know what you mean!*

Justin probably thought he was sounding artistic and soulful. But he was actually sounding like the most depressed person on earth! *I don't talk like that,* Daniel thought. *Do I?*

'Justin?' Riley's voice snapped him out of his agony.

'Yeah . . . I am Justin.' Daniel looked up to find her looking worried.

'You don't like that idea?' she asked.

'Ah . . .' Desperately, Daniel tried to remember what she'd just said. He'd been so busy listening to Justin and Debi, he hadn't heard a word.

Groaning silently, Daniel admitted the truth to himself: He was just no good at dates . . . even the ones that weren't his own!

How had he *ever* thought that he could date Debi?

※　　　　※　　　　※

On the other side of the diner, Justin tried not to grimace as he took the tiniest possible bite of Daniel's club sandwich. *I can't believe he left it all for me to eat!* After the huge burger and fries he'd scarfed down in his own booth, he was pretty sure his stomach would explode if he forced down any more.

This is a complete disaster, he thought. From the look on Debi's face, he was ninety-nine per cent sure he was only *hurting* his brother's chances with her, not helping Daniel after all.

At least she hadn't walked out . . . yet. But, from the expression on her face, Justin worried she was giving it some thought.

19

'So . . .' She took a deep breath. 'Can you recommend any good bands for me to listen to? Ones that you like?'

'Um . . .' Justin hesitated.

He'd never been any good at pretending he knew *anything* about music. All those songs that Daniel played non-stop at home were just noise to Justin – he had no idea who any of the bands were. The all sounded the same – miserable, angry, and very eager to shout about it.

'I . . . like . . . stuff that rocks,' he said, and tried his best to scowl artistically. Unfortunately, he was pretty sure he just looked like his stomach hurt . . . which it did. How much more of Daniel's meal could he force down?

'Like . . .?' Debi prompted.

'Uh . . .' In desperation, Justin stuffed the club sandwich back into his mouth, even as his stomach screamed in protest. He had to buy the time to think somehow! *Come on, brain! Last night Mom asked Daniel what he'd been listening to, and Daniel said . . . He said . . .*

Nope, it was useless. Justin had tuned out of that whole conversation, too busy thinking about the Homecoming Game. He and Dad had ended up in a big debate over training tactics while Mom and Daniel had talked music.

Oh, great, Justin thought. *I'm going to have to eat this whole sandwich just to have an excuse not to talk!*

Then something caught his attention on the other side of the room, and he had to stifle a moan of relief.

Daniel was stoop-walking out of the Meat & Greet, just like last time, pausing only long enough to signal in Justin's direction.

Justin dropped the sandwich back on to its plate. 'Sorry, I'll be right back. I've just gotta . . .' He gestured vaguely, hoping she would think up an explanation for herself.

'That's fine,' Debi said, and sighed. 'Really. Totally fine.'

Uh-oh. Justin grimaced as he hurried away. *Anyone who says they're 'fine' twice in the same breath is never 'fine'.*

A minute later, he was pulling off Daniel's scruffy band shirt and buttoning his own shirt back up with relief. Unfortunately . . .

'Hey!' said Justin. 'You've got it all creased!'

'That's probably from the stoop-walking.' Daniel shrugged as he pulled on his own shirt again. 'Mine's probably creased, too. So what?'

'But no one can tell with *yours*.' Justin shook his head and did his best to smooth down his shirt. 'Whatever. I'm just glad to be heading back where I belong. Seriously, dude, don't ever ask me to do that again.'

'I won't.' Daniel grimaced. 'Trust me. But

look!' He held out his arm. 'I'm all back to normal again. No fur! So, thanks – you really did save me.'

'Yeah,' Justin said, doing his best to look confident. 'Saved you. That's what I did. Yep. Although, I think you should start talking about your favourite bands – Debi seems really keen for some recommendations.'

'Awesome – that's conversation I'm actually good at!'

By the time he slid back into the seat across from Riley a minute later, Justin was more than ready to call the not-a-date over. 'Hey, do you want to get out of here?'

'What?' Riley's head jerked up from the stack of clipboards she'd been studying. While Justin had been gone, they'd somehow multiplied from two to four. Now she ignored them all to stare at him in open shock. 'You want to leave already? I thought we were having dessert. Your stomach was rumbling just a minute ago — and they make the best ice cream in town here!'

'Uh . . .'

Justin's stomach gurgled warningly. *Warning! Warning! Explosion imminent!*

Riley's brown eyes were fixed on him. He swallowed hard, fighting back a groan. He knew how much she loved ice cream.

'Of course,' he mumbled, and sank down in the seat, giving up. 'I just forgot.'

'Oh, good!' Riley said.

Justin put on his best fake smile as he signalled for the waitress. 'Two sundaes, please!'

'Large ones,' added Riley.

Riley went back to doodling quickly on one of the clipboards, while Justin tried to prepare himself for *more food.*

This was what sappy singers meant every time they sang '*love hurts*'.

Chapter Two

As soon as the twins were safely home and alone, Daniel headed straight for the kitchen. 'Finally. I thought I'd never make it back here!' He tore into the refrigerator, searching for sandwich fillings.

'*I* can't believe you're eating *more*.' Justin collapsed on to a chair at the kitchen table, closing his eyes. 'After everything we had at the Meat & Greet?'

'Everything *you* had,' Daniel corrected. He sat down opposite Justin and started to spread mustard and mayonnaise over his sandwich bread, salivating at the smells. 'You'd already eaten your burger by the time I took over for you, remember? And by the time I got back to my table, Debi had asked the waitress to clear the plates! Apparently . . .' he gave Justin a meaningful glance as he slapped in the cold cuts, '. . . she somehow got the impression I had no appetite!'

'Argh.' Justin tipped his head on to the table with a groan. 'You don't know how lucky you are. Riley thought I was ravenous! I know I wanted to bulk up for football, but at this rate, I'll be able to try out for the Sumo team instead!'

Daniel snickered, imagining it. 'You're out of luck,' he said, through his mouthful of sandwich. 'Pine Wood doesn't have a Sumo team.'

Justin gave him a narrow-eyed look. 'This is no time to be literal. I'm dying here, Bro!'

'A large sundae never killed anybody.' Daniel

grinned as he took another bite. 'Maybe I should take a picture to send to the school paper: the big tough football player slain by his first date.'

'Don't call it that!' Justin's eyes flew open. He jerked upright, looking outraged. 'It was a not-a-date. And, anyway –'

Before he could say another word, though, the kitchen door opened. 'There you are!' It was their dad, dressed in a ragged grey sweatsuit. He looked like a guy in a 70s boxing movie – he even wore a green headband. 'I've been searching for you everywhere!'

It took a moment before Daniel realised his dad was staring right at him.

'Me?' Daniel blinked, taking another bite of his sandwich. 'Are you sure you weren't looking for Justin? If you want someone to help with your marathon training, he's really the one –'

'No, no, no!' Dad shook his head. Half his

hair was sticking up as if he'd been caught in a hurricane – or had been tugging at it with his fingers. 'You need to be ready. There's going to be a *gathering* tomorrow night.'

'A what?' Daniel asked, sharing a confused look with Justin.

'A gathering of *Lupines*!' Dad said impatiently. 'I have to bring my son the werewolf!'

'Oh.' Daniel swallowed hard. *Uh-oh. I guess he did mean me, after all.*

Daniel might have been a werewolf for nearly a month, but that didn't mean he was comfortable with it at all. He could barely even control his own werewolf powers yet. The idea of being completely surrounded by other werewolves, doing . . . well, whatever they did at those 'gatherings' . . .

He had to force himself not to shiver.

'Oh, what a shame,' Daniel said, forcing an

upbeat tone, 'I'm afraid I've already got plans for tomorrow night. My band –'

Dad fixed him with a hard stare. 'This isn't optional, Daniel. Like it or not, you are one of us, and you need to attend these gatherings. They are *essential* if you want to master your new abilities and learn about your heritage.'

'My what?' Daniel winced, trying not to look at Justin. *We're twins. We can't have different heritages!* 'I'm part-human, too, remember?'

'That makes it all the more important.' Dad pointed a warning finger at him. 'It is *only* by spending time with the wolves that you will be able to fit in better with the humans. Do you understand?'

No, Daniel thought. Then, as he looked down to avoid his dad's disappointed eyes, he caught sight of his own arm . . . which reminded him of this afternoon's disastrous, *hair-raising* date.

Learning how to not suddenly sprout wolf-fur probably wasn't the *worst* idea in the world.

'OK,' he said, sighing. 'I'll go.'

As Dad hurried back out of the room to make some calls, Daniel stared down at the sandwich in his hand. Two minutes ago he'd been starving, but now he set the sandwich down on his plate and looked at Justin. But his twin was gazing down at the table, shoulders sagging.

Maybe it was Justin's stomach making him feel bad . . . or maybe he felt bad about something completely different.

Up until a month ago, Justin was the one who'd had all the intense, secret conversations and hang-outs with their dad. He was the one who'd expected to take part in all of this. Meanwhile, Daniel had never even known werewolves were real until the first time he'd looked in the mirror and seen a wolf's face where his should have been.

'Hey,' Daniel said. He cleared his throat awkwardly, pushing his sandwich around. 'Are you OK?'

'Me?' Justin frowned as he looked up. 'Why wouldn't I be?'

'Well . . .' Daniel picked up his sandwich, then set it down again, sighing. 'I just don't want you to feel left out.'

'I'm fine, Bro.' Justin shrugged. 'Totally fine.'

Anyone who says they're 'fine' twice in the same breath is never *'fine',* Daniel thought. 'You sure?' he asked.

'Yeah,' said Justin. 'I've got enough going on, with Homecoming coming up, and . . . school . . . and everything. I'm sorry to miss that gathering, though. It sounds fun.'

Daniel stared at him, trying to put together the concepts of *'fun'* and *'werewolf gathering'*. But it didn't work. His body still clenched with dread at

31

the whole thought of it. 'Are you serious?'

'Heck, yeah.' Justin gave his usual confident grin. 'Hanging out with a bunch of werewolves, using all your super-strength to push yourself to your limits – what could be better?'

'Right,' Daniel said flatly. 'Total fun.' He tried to smile back, but he couldn't. He'd just made a seriously depressing realisation.

My brother is a better werewolf than I am, he thought. *And he's human!*

The next morning, Justin was waiting with the rest of the football team outside the school auditorium. An assembly was about to start and, for once, Justin couldn't wait – because he desperately needed a distraction, *now*. Otherwise he might just be sick!

Of course he knew that the werewolf players on the football team – known collectively as the Beasts – liked to eat rare meat in their sandwiches. But did they *really* have to carry it around with them everywhere? At first he'd thought he was imagining the smell. Then he'd spotted the rare burger sticking out of Ed Yancey's pocket, and stumbled back away from the stench. *No way can that be hygienic!*

Trying to hide his revulsion, Justin turned away – and found Kyle Hunter, the leader of the Beasts, looking at him knowingly. 'Hungry, Packer?' Kyle reached into the pocket of his football jacket. 'Want a bite of my beef to tide you over? It's from a couple of days back but –'

'No, thanks.' Justin fought down nausea. As far as the Beasts knew, Justin was a werewolf just like them. *If I threw up on his shoes that would definitely give my secret away.* The last thing he wanted was for them to find out the truth.

'Maybe later,' Justin said weakly. 'I just ate a full side of bacon . . . two, actually.' But he couldn't help swallowing hard as the smell of the *old,* raw meat floated up to him.

'Ha!' Ed Yancey chortled. 'I saw that, Packer! Getting a little . . . "light-headed"?'

'Um . . . Err . . .' Justin panicked. *How could they tell?*

Ed elbowed him, smirking. 'I saw who was walking past just then. I think our running back has a crush!'

'What?' Justin yelped. He had to force himself not to spin around and look. Was Riley nearby? Was she watching? *Is my hair OK?*

As he reached up to check that it was smooth, the other Beasts burst into raucous laughter.

'I'd never have guessed it!' Kyle said, and

smacked Justin on the back. 'So, Justin likes the cheerleading style, huh?'

'I do?' Justin stared at him, caught off-guard.

'Yup.' Kyle shook his head, grinning. 'I never would have thought Mackenzie Barton was your type.'

'*What?!*' Justin stared at him. 'You're kidding, right?'

Mackenzie Barton was the head of the cheerleading team – and Pine Wood Junior High's reigning Queen of Mean. Justin and Daniel had lived across the street from her for years before she'd finally moved to a different side of town.

Justin still didn't know why they hadn't had a huge party that day.

'I would never . . . I'm not . . .'

'He's stuttering,' Chris Jackson said, grinning. 'You know what that means. He has a *thang* for Mackenzie.'

'Argh!' Justin started to turn away – and caught sight of Riley staring at him from the edge of the crowd.

She had definitely been close enough to hear what the Beasts were saying. *Oh, no!*

Justin whirled back around. 'Shut up!' he hissed. 'Seriously, guys. Please! Don't say another word!'

'Aha!' Ed beamed, looking as if he'd made the most hilarious joke ever. 'That's proof. We definitely hit a nerve. You definitely like Mackenzie!'

Panic made Justin's thoughts veer and crash together like bumper cars. He knew his team mates wouldn't stop teasing him until he admitted something. But the only way out of this would be to admit the truth about who he *really* liked. And he couldn't do that while she was in earshot.

Why does it have to be such a big deal just to like *a girl?* he asked himself desperately.

Then he saw who was walking towards them through the crowd. Groaning, he tried to close his eyes . . . But he couldn't look away from his doom.

Why? Why is everything bad in the whole world happening to me?

Mackenzie Barton was walking straight towards him, her ponytail swishing around the shoulders of her cheerleading jacket.

'I've gotta go,' Justin mumbled. 'I'll be right –'

'Absolutely not!' Kyle clamped a vice-like hand on Justin's shoulder, holding him trapped. 'Trust me, Packer. You can do this! We've got your back.'

The other Beasts crowded around, snickering and wolf-whistling.

Justin saw Riley watching from the edge of the crowd. His stomach sank.

Mackenzie sauntered to a stop directly in front

of him, smiling sweetly and batting her eyelids. The bizarre sight made Justin's breath speed up with panic.

Why is she smiling at me like that? Is this a trick?

'Hey, Justin,' she said, her voice all light and fluttery. 'How are you doing?'

Justin gulped, feeling Riley's eyes on him.

Mackenzie had *never* asked him how he was doing before. As far as he could tell, she'd never cared about how anyone was doing, apart from herself!

'Fine, thank you. And you?' She batted her lashes even more rapidly. 'Have you got something in your eye?'

'Oh, I'm fine,' Mackenzie said, stopping the mad fluttering and leaning a little closer. 'I just wanted to wish you luck for the upcoming game – and to tell you that you should try to avoid getting injured in practice.'

'Oh. Thanks for . . . "caring",' he said.

'It would suck for Pine Wood's Homecoming King to be limping around on Coronation Day!'

What?!

Justin was still gaping at her when the doors of the auditorium finally swung open. He'd never been so relieved to be swept along with the crowd as they stampeded inside, carrying him away from Mackenzie.

Normal, mean Mackenzie was bad enough. He knew how to deal with her in her usual moods. *Duck and cover!* But a Mackenzie who was trying to be *friendly* . . . that couldn't signal anything good.

And what had she meant about Homecoming King?

He tried to look anywhere but at the smirking faces of Kyle, Ed, Chris, and the rest of the Beasts as they took their places at the front of the auditorium.

Up on stage, Principal Caine was already waiting for them. She may have been smaller than some of her students, with pale grey hair and eyes, but none of that diminished her icy fierceness – or the intensity of her glare, which could paralyse even the Beasts at their rowdiest. When she stepped up to the podium and called for quiet, an immediate hush swept across the auditorium.

'Thank you, students,' she said. 'Now! I would like to formally announce the upcoming Homecoming Game and Dance.'

The auditorium erupted. Excited chatter swept through the audience of girls, while the Beasts rose up in their seats to hoot and holler:

'Pine Wood! Pine Wood! Pine Wood!'

Justin smirked as he looked across the auditorium to see Daniel and his band mates Otto and Nathan all sitting together. The only ones who didn't seem excited . . . *Yup. I knew it.*

Daniel was looking pointedly at the ceiling with his arms crossed in open resistance; Otto sprawled across his seat, as though bored; and Nathan sat yawning and rubbing his eyes.

Justin smiled. *So much for 'School Spirit'!*

'Ahem,' said Principal Caine, and the noise died down. Her face tightened as she said grimly, 'I am certain we are all looking forward to the festivities.'

Yeah, right. Justin bit back a laugh. From the look on Principal Caine's face, she might have just bitten into a prune. *Has she ever looked forward to anything, ever?*

'One very lucky student band will be allowed to perform their music to their peers at the Dance,' Principal Caine continued. 'Auditions will be held tomorrow after school, and we invite all bands to sign up for this educational event.'

41

She shook her head irritably. 'Otherwise, there won't be much of a competition! At the moment, we only have one band on our list: *In Pig's* . . . I beg your pardon.' She squinted at the paper in her hands. 'I mean, *In Sheep's Clothing*, of course.'

No way! Justin choked on his laughter. Still fighting for breath, he swivelled in his seat to check out Daniel and the others.

Nathan was clutching at his throat, Otto was making gagging motions . . . and Daniel looked like he'd just lived through a live-action horror film.

They had no idea they'd entered, Justin realised, as he looked at his brother's stunned expression. *Uh-oh.* He smirked to himself. *I bet I know exactly who did it.*

As he turned back towards the stage, he caught Riley gesturing across the auditorium to the others, mouthing: *I'll explain later.*

I knew it. Justin grinned. He hoped he'd be around for *that* explanation.

'Miss Carter?' Principal Caine's voice clipped out sharply, making Riley jerk back around in her seat. 'Do you have a question?'

'No, ma'am.' Riley beamed at her.

'Are you sure?' Principal Caine raised her eyebrows sternly. 'Surely you wouldn't be waving your arms around for any other reason?'

'No, ma'am,' Riley repeated obediently. She folded her hands on top of the pile of notebooks on her lap.

Justin could tell she was trying to sit still – but, being Riley, that was a lost cause. She was practically wriggling with impatience to get moving and organising!

'Hmm.' Principal Caine gave her a long look before moving on. 'Voting for Homecoming King and Queen will commence today and close by the end of the week. I am sure . . .' her face hardened into stone, '. . . that we are all very excited about this.'

Justin snorted. *If this is her version of excited, I'd hate to see her when she's depressed!*

'There will be a table in the cafeteria where you may all cast your votes. Of course, we'll need someone to organise the voting and I'm extending an open invitation to anyone who wishes to take on this responsibility.'

A hush fell over the auditorium, as hundreds of hands stayed firmly by their sides. All except one.

Principal Caine looked in every direction but to her left, where she would have seen Riley almost standing up, trying to make herself seen. Finally, the Principal sighed: 'Fine, Miss Carter. The job is yours.'

'Thank you, ma'am!' Riley chirped. She

immediately flipped open her top notebook and began to scribble.

Principal Caine cleared her throat as she picked up a new sheet of paper. 'And now to announce the nominations for Homecoming King.'

Uh-oh. Justin stiffened in his seat. If Mackenzie was right . . .

'Caleb Devlin,' Principal Caine read, in a carrying voice. 'Kyle Hunter, Justin Packer . . .'

Oh, no. Justin's heart sank. *That's why Mackenzie was being nice to me!* As the rest of the list of names was read out, Justin met his twin's eyes across the crowded auditorium.

Daniel shook his head in obvious disgust. *Uh-oh*, Justin thought. *I know that look.* It was an expression Justin usually only saw from his brother when he got the name of a 'very significant' album wrong.

What could I do? Justin shrugged and turned

up his hands in a helpless gesture. He'd had no control over the nominations!

Daniel's eyes narrowed. But then the principal cleared her throat again.

'And now for the Homecoming Queen nominations . . .'

Justin closed his eyes. *Please, please, please, not . . .*

'The first candidate is Mackenzie Barton,' Principal Caine read. 'And the second candidate . . .'

But her voice was covered up by the victorious shrieking of Mackenzie, and – a second later – the echo of her entourage. It was so deafening, Justin covered his ears, scrunching down in his seat to escape. Even sitting at the front of the auditorium, he couldn't quite catch the second name on the list.

Principal Caine shook her head, giving Mackenzie a stern look. 'If we could have some quiet, please, Miss Barton? The third and final nominee for Homecoming Queen is . . . Debi Morgan!'

Ha! Justin grinned straight at his brother. Under his breath, he mumbled: 'Bet you don't think it's lame now, do you?'

Daniel glared at Justin. Then Justin realised, Daniel had heard him all the way across the auditorium. 'I forgot you have super-strong hearing now,' said Justin, grinning. 'This is going to be fun!'

As the assembly finally ended, Daniel shuffled along with the crowd filing out of the auditorium. His thoughts were miles away, on the gathering that would be happening that night.

What exactly happened at a werewolf

gathering? Dad had refused to give him any hints, no matter how hard he pestered. But when he tried to imagine it for himself . . .

Someone grabbed his arm, and he let out a yip of surprise.

Oops. He slammed his mouth shut, just a moment too late. *I hope no one heard that!* It had definitely sounded . . . *cub*-like!

Luckily, his band mates were still too depressed about Homecoming to notice. 'Walk with me!' Justin whispered, yanking on his arm.

'Why?' Daniel asked, pulling back.

Justin made a face. 'Because Mackenzie Barton is a lot less likely to approach me if I'm surrounded by you and your Band of Moody Men!'

Laughing, Daniel fell into step. Justin had a point – Otto and Nathan did look pretty moody at that moment.

'Since when are you scared of Mackenzie?' he asked.

Justin looked agonised. 'Ever since she got it into her head that Pine Wood needs its very own Kate and William.'

'Who?' Daniel shook his head, baffled.

'Dude, you *seriously* need to at least take a peek at mainstream news every once in a while.' Justin rolled his eyes. 'There's being alternative, and then there's just being *clueless*.'

'Oh, shut up.' Daniel elbowed him, grinning. 'So what is it, exactly, that Mackenzie wants from you?'

Justin groaned. 'She thinks we're going to be Homecoming King and Queen!'

'I can see you two together,' said Daniel, with a nod.

'I seriously need help,' said Justin. 'And I thought, who better than you to ask how to kill girls' interest? You've been doing it naturally for so long!'

'It is a gift,' Daniel said solemnly. 'Either you've got it, or you don't. And I can't help you if you lack the natural skills.'

For a moment, they laughed, but Justin then gave Daniel a shove. 'Don't make me laugh – I shouldn't be laughing. This is crisis-time.'

'OK, OK.' Daniel forced himself to think it through as they neared their classrooms. The crowd in the hallway was already starting to thin as other students disappeared into their next classes. 'Look, I can't help you out of this one. If she's elected Homecoming Queen and you're elected Homecoming King . . .'

Justin looked like he had had a touchdown disallowed, or something. 'Then I'm trapped. We'll have to *dance* at Homecoming together.'

'Unless . . .' Daniel frowned, hesitating a few

feet away from the door of his next class. 'Who says Mackenzie *has* to win? If she loses, you're free and clear.'

'Oh, come on.' Justin fell back against the wall of lockers, looking miserable. 'Mackenzie was the Queen Bee at middle school, and she'll probably be *Empress* Bee here. Who could possibly take her on?'

Daniel looked down at his boots. 'I dunno, Bro.'

He heard Justin gasp. 'Debi!'

'Where?' Daniel looked around, but couldn't see her anywhere. Then he finally got it. 'Debi for Homecoming Queen? That's brilliant. She's new, she's pretty, she's fun, she's lovely. She has a smile that could . . .' Daniel stopped himself before he turned wolf. He took a deep breath. 'I think she could beat Mackenzie if she tried.'

Hey, she could do anything, he thought . . . But he didn't say that. No way was he going to sound that sappy in front of his brother. Did he have a cheesy grin on his face, just from thinking about her? *Uh-oh*. He was pretty sure he did.

'So, you'll talk to her about it?' Justin said.

'What?' Daniel choked, his grin disappearing. 'I didn't say that!'

'Come on, dude!' Justin grabbed his arm. 'You have to help me out. If Debi wants to win, she has to *campaign* for it. She can't just sit back and let Mackenzie roll all over her. You need to talk her into *fighting for the crown*!'

'Uh . . .' Daniel winced. 'You know how I feel about the whole Homecoming thing. And after yesterday's mess at the Meat & Greet, I honestly don't know if Debi even wants to talk to me about anything.'

'*Please*, Bro. I'm asking you to save me!' Justin dropped to his knees in the middle of the hallway, throwing out his arms in a melodramatic gesture. 'You can't let me be Mackenzinated!'

'All right, fine . . .' Daniel sighed. 'Just get up off the floor, before Coach Johnston thinks you've injured your TCL.'

'You mean ACL,' said Justin, jumping to his feet.

'I'll do my best,' said Daniel, 'but I can't make any promises. Seriously, after yesterday, she probably thinks I'm a total weirdo.'

'Then you can't make things any worse,' Justin said. He brushed himself off, grinning, and started to saunter away towards his next classroom. 'Right?'

Daniel winced. 'Is that your impersonation of an encouraging little brother?'

'Sorry, dude.' Justin paused, turning back. 'Um . . . good luck?'

'Thanks,' Daniel said dryly, and turned towards the doorway of his own next class.

Behind him, he heard Justin mumble: 'Who you calling "little" brother?'

An hour later, Daniel stood in the cafeteria doorway, took a deep breath and . . . immediately regretted it. His werewolf senses picked up every single smell in the cafeteria and the kitchen beyond – and probably the alley behind the school where the trash was dumped. *Yuck!*

At least he had a packed lunch. Taking shallow breaths to hold out the stink, he started towards Debi's table. It was easy to find: her bright red hair shone like a beacon, summoning him across the room. Even the thought of having to walk up to a table occupied *completely* by girls wasn't enough to slow him down.

Unfortunately, within thirty yards of Debi's table, he could hear exactly the wrong kind of conversation taking place.

'No, seriously!' Debi was saying to the girls around her. 'I'm just happy to be nominated for Homecoming Queen, especially since I'm new in town. That's just cool.' She smiled and took a sip of her orange juice. 'I don't need any more than that.'

'Yeah, but come on, Debi!' The girl on her left, Sarah Perkins, shook her head. 'Don't you want to *win*?'

Debi shrugged and unwrapped her lunch. 'Nah, not really.'

'But why not?' The girl on her right, Eileen Black, let out a groan of longing. 'Just think of it! The crown, the dance, the pictures, getting treated like a queen for a whole week . . . *and* showing Mackenzie that she can't win at everything!'

'That's the main problem.' Debi sighed. 'I've got enough to deal with on the cheerleading team already, without irritating Mackenzie even more.'

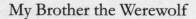

Oh, no. Daniel cringed, stopping still in the middle of the cafeteria as he absorbed her words. *I'm going to look like a total idiot if I butt in and tell her to do just that!*

He almost turned around – but then he caught sight of Justin across the room. He was sitting at a table full of football players, most of them busy with a messy food fight – but Justin wasn't paying any attention. The pleading puppy expression on his face was impossible to ignore.

Daniel squared his shoulders as he headed into danger. He couldn't let his brother be Mackenzinated . . . even if he did have to get involved with *Homecoming* to save him!

The horror . . .

As he approached Debi's table, Daniel put on his best 'confident grin'. Sticking his hands in his pockets, he nodded politely to the other girls, then turned to Debi. He hadn't talked to her since yesterday's debacle at the Meat & Greet, but – thank goodness – she smiled at him just as brightly as if that had never happened. *Maybe she'll give me another chance . . . if I don't mess this up too badly!*

'Hey,' he said. 'Are you excited about the nomination?'

As if I didn't already know the answer.

'I'm just happy to be nominated,' Debi said. She must have practised her answer, because it came out exactly as he'd heard it only moments ago. His spirits sank as he heard her say the familiar words: 'Especially since I'm new. That's –'

'–"Just cool",' Daniel finished for her, glumly. 'Right.' He sighed.

Then he saw the expression on her face. She was staring at him. 'How did you know what I was going to say?'

He froze. *Back away! Don't let her know you're a*

freaky furball boy with super-hearing! 'I . . . That's how I would feel if *I . . .*'

'Got nominated for Homecoming Queen?' asked Sarah Perkins. The whole table erupted with a fit of giggles that threatened to knock him off his feet.

Debi was clearly stifling a laugh, too.

Maybe Justin was right; Daniel really didn't have much experience with girls who actually liked him. But he was pretty sure he recognised the look on Debi's face right now, and he could tell she was thinking that he might have been the weirdest boy she had ever met.

He cringed. Between yesterday and today, how much worse of an impression could he make? He could practically hear the warning bells jangling in his brain. *Red alert! Red alert! Run now, before it's too late!*

Lowering his head in an idiotic nod, he started

to turn to make his getaway. Then a familiar voice sounded in his ear: Justin, whispering to him from all the way on the other side of the cafeteria.

'*Do* not *lose your nerve, Bro. Remember what's at stake!*'

Daniel winced. It was hardly fair that Justin literally got to be a voice-in-his-head! Sometimes werewolf super-senses were anything *but* an advantage.

Still, he steeled himself to turn back to Debi. 'I think you'd be a *great* Homecoming Queen,' he said, through gritted teeth.

'You do?' Debi blinked at him, while the other girls looked shocked then started whispering to each other. 'I thought you hated Homecoming!'

'Well . . .' Daniel winced. 'I know I'm not really a fan in general, but –'

'Yesterday at the Meat & Greet, you said you thought the whole King and Queen deal was

59

lame.' Debi frowned at him. 'What's changed?'

'Well – well, it's not that – it's more . . .' Daniel sighed, and gave up. All he had left was . . . the truth. 'You *have* to be the Queen,' he said, sinking down on to the seat next to her. 'If you don't win, then Mackenzie will. And she'll be a nightmare.'

'He's so right,' Eileen said. She gave Daniel an approving look even as she spoke to Debi. 'You know she'll take her "Queen" role way too seriously. Everyone will suffer under her . . . regime.'

On Debi's left, Sarah rolled her eyes. 'I bet she already has a tiara on mail order. And that she's planning to wear it for the whole week that she's Queen.'

'It'll be a reign of terror!' Eileen gasped.

Debi gave a sigh. 'I'm sure you're right. But still . . .' She shrugged helplessly. 'What can *I* do? I just don't have it in me to campaign for votes.

If people like me, they like me. If they don't, they don't. So . . .?' She held out her hands. 'Anyway, titles and popularity don't really matter, do they?'

She kept going, but Daniel couldn't focus. Inwardly, he was smiling. He couldn't agree more.

But then Justin's voice was mumbling in his ear again. *'You're losing her. Try harder!'*

Daniel hunched his shoulders. 'Shut up!' he growled at his brother . . .

. . . and Debi's eyes widened with shock. 'Excuse me?'

'Sorry!' Daniel stood up quickly, horrified. 'I wasn't . . .'

I wasn't what? Daniel thought. *Wasn't talking to her? Who else could I have been talking to?*

'. . . I just . . .'

Think, Packer. Think!

'I didn't mean "shut up" as in "be quiet",'

61

he garbled. 'I meant, "shut up" as in: *Shuuuuut uuuuup.*' He put on his girliest voice. 'You are, like, so *totally* going to win. Completely. Posalutely.'

Now you're just making up words!

'Posalutely?' asked Debi, with a frown. 'I don't know . . .'

'What if someone else campaigned for you?' Daniel said, hoping to change the subject – and quick.

Debi laughed. 'Who would even want to do that?' Shaking her head, she gestured at herself. 'Come on, Daniel. Nobody even knows me well enough to run around the school telling everyone how amazing I am.'

'I do.' The words had come out before Daniel could stop them.

Eileen and Sarah's jaws dropped so fast, they might have needed parachutes.

Daniel could feel the tingle of his teeth. His

incisors were growing, right there at the cafeteria table. 'I mean . . . I mean . . .' he said. He only just managed to turn away before he said: 'I mean, *I do* . . . very much think we could find someone to do that for you.'

Luckily, the girls at the table all started talking. They were so quick that even with his werewolf hearing he couldn't work out what they were saying. They didn't seem to have the same problem, though, and within a minute they'd made some kind of agreement.

'Definitely,' said Eileen, with a firm nod. 'Riley Carter is the only one capable of pulling this off.'

Debi bit her lip, looking thoughtful. 'Maybe. But Riley's organising the Homecoming Game *and* the Homecoming Dance. When would she have any time left to help me out?'

'Hey, it doesn't hurt to ask, right?' said Daniel,

and grinned. He knew just the guy who could ask for Riley's help.

It's payback time, Bro.

Chapter Three

Half an hour later, Justin was standing in his English class, feeling as nervous as if he were about to run on-field for a big game. *Get a grip, cub!* he ordered himself. *You can do this.*

Slowly, reluctantly, he forced his feet to move across the floor. Since everyone was working on individual projects, the room felt unnaturally quiet, with only a soft hum of conversations in between some of the desks. His loud, clomping footsteps sounded like thunder in his ears. With every step, he was certain that people would look up at him and demand to know *what* he was doing.

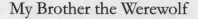

Halfway to Riley's desk, he stalled, panicking. Maybe if he waited until later . . .

No, he told himself firmly. *Daniel asked Debi, so I have to ask Riley.* Plus, anything had to be better than being Mackenzie Barton's King! The thought was so gruesome, its force pushed him all the way to Riley's desk.

There, there was the final barrier: the piles of stacked papers and files that formed a gate between Riley and the world.

Just be cool, Justin ordered himself. *Be cool, be cool . . .*

'Justin?' Riley looked up at him, blinking. 'Is everything OK?'

'Uh . . .' *Oh, no.* How long had he been standing – no, *looming* – there without saying a word? *Looming is probably not cool!* 'I – I just – I mean . . .' *Aaagh!*

Justin slapped himself mentally. *Come on! You*

do know some *words in the English language!*

The words blurted themselves out in a rush: 'I wondered if you wanted to help Debi's campaign to be Homecoming Queen!' *Phew. That wasn't so bad.*

Except that Riley was looking at him as if he was crazier than someone who was wearing paisley with plaid. Justin didn't really know what that meant, but he knew it meant *super*-crazy.

Re-group, re-group! 'It would just be cool,' he followed up, 'if Mackenzie didn't walk to victory, for once. Don't you think?'

Riley rolled her eyes at him. '*Really*, Justin?' Riley was still looking at him as if he was insane. Had Justin scored the most depressing two-fer in Pine Wood history – ruining things for himself *and* his brother in one conversation? 'Did you seriously think you even had to ask?'

Justin's shoulders relaxed. He gave her a

grin. 'You mean I didn't have to?'

She grinned back. 'I've already come up with a strategy.'

Justin shook his head. 'That's amazing! How did you know Debi would be campaigning?'

She shrugged. 'I didn't. I just like to be prepared in case I am ever called upon.'

Justin tried to keep the goofy grin off his face, but it was hard when Riley was being so . . . *Riley*. 'When did you even have time to put it together?'

'You'd be surprised what you can do when you ignore the need for sleep!'

Justin pointed at her piles of paper. 'Can I see it?'

Still smiling, Riley tapped her head. 'It's all up here – oops!' As she tapped, she knocked a hairpin loose. One side of her long blonde hair tumbled free, all the way down over her shoulder.

Justin stared, his throat suddenly feeling as dry

as if he hadn't drunk any water for days.

Riley laughed as she scooped up her hairpin. 'I'm not sure this new look is entirely working for me . . .'

'Uhh . . .' Justin tried to think of something – *anything* – smart to say as he watched her scoop up the wave of shining blonde hair from her shoulder.

He couldn't.

All he could do was hope that she couldn't hear his heart beating . . . very, very loudly.

'Anyway . . .' Riley flashed him a smile as she settled the hairpin firmly back in place. 'I'll write my plans down later. You can see them once I'm done. OK?'

Be cool. Be cool!

It was a lost cause. 'Uh,' said Justin. 'Uhhh. Yeah. Great! Super!'

Then he turned and fled back towards his

desk. He vowed that, if time-travel was ever invented, he would come back to this very moment and stop his younger self from saying 'Super!' in front of Riley.

He had never in his life been so relieved to sit down. Unfortunately, Daniel was at the desk right in front of him. Justin's twin turned and grinned at him. 'So . . .' he whispered. 'That's some techno rhythm your heart's beating out right now, huh?'

Justin scowled at his brother. *Werewolf hearing sucks!* But before he could answer, someone bumped hard against his shoulder. 'Hey!'

It was Milo, the guy who'd competed against Riley earlier that month for the position of lead singer for *In Sheep's Clothing*. He bounced off Justin's shoulder, landed almost right on top of Daniel's desk, and finally fell headlong on to the ground.

'Are you OK?' Justin asked. He started to his feet.

Daniel reached down to help, too. 'Here, let me —'

'Leave me alone!' Milo shook Daniel off, wrapping his arms around his chest. 'I'm fine, and I definitely don't want *your* help, Packer!'

'Ohhh-kaaaaay . . .' Daniel sat back, shaking his head.

Justin sighed as he watched Milo stomp off to his own desk. *I guess he's still pretty sore about not getting the gig in Daniel's band.*

Really, though . . . Justin shook his head as he sat back down. What else could Daniel have done? Riley was a better singer than Milo. Riley was a better everything than Milo. Riley was better than everyone! She was just so . . . so . . .

. . . *So looking straight at me!*

With a jolt, Justin suddenly realised that he'd

71

been gazing at Riley for at least a full minute . . . and she was looking back at him with a mixture of concern and confusion on her face.

Justin jerked his head to look down at his desk. He had a horrible feeling that he'd been gazing at her adoringly. *Argh!*

As embarrassment burned through his body, a small voice inside him wondered: why did it always seem so *vital* that the girl he liked never actually found out that he liked her?

It was a question he still hadn't answered three hours later, as he walked into his house after football practice. By then, though, he was starting to feel better about the whole thing. Slinging his jacket on to a hook, he raced upstairs to his bedroom, charged with excitement.

Computers will save me!

Maybe he couldn't talk like a normal person

in front of Riley, nowadays. But at least he could work with her online to get Debi elected Homecoming Queen. And best of all, when he was typing all his words online, no one could hear him saying 'Uhhh' over and over again, like he was a malfunctioning droid from a Cole Knightley sci-fi book.

He flung his backpack on to his bed and hurried to the computer on his desk. Maybe he'd make such a good impression on Riley online that she would forget all about the weirdness at the Meat & Greet yesterday. And in English class today. And maybe . . .

At the sound of a muffled crash, he looked around. *Was that Daniel?*

'Aargh!'

That was definitely his brother's yelp, coming from the bedroom next door – and it was followed by a second massive crash.

Justin hurried through their shared bathroom and opened the inner door to Daniel's room. His eyes widened as he took in the sight before him.

'Wow,' he said. 'Did you get burgled?'

'Very funny.' Daniel glared at him from the middle of the floor, where he sat on his knees surrounded by up-ended drawers, clothes and piles of paper. 'I'm fine, OK? Everything's fine.'

'If you say so.' Justin looked around the disaster zone that his brother's bedroom had become. 'So . . . can I ask why your room looks like it's just hosted a kung-fu rumble?'

'It's nothing,' Daniel said. He crossed his arms and tried to look casual. Any time that Daniel tried to look casual, it never came off.

Justin shook his head. 'Try again, Bro. No way would you destroy this place for something that's "nothing". Not to mention the yelping I heard.'

'I wasn't yelping!'

'I'm still wai-ting . . .' Justin sung.

Daniel sighed and closed his eyes. 'OK. So, you know Dad wants me to go to that "gathering" tonight . . .? I just wanted to find something before I went. But I've lost it.'

'I'll help you look.' Justin stepped inside the room, closing the door behind him. 'What is it?'

Daniel looked away quickly, but Justin still caught the embarrassed flush on his brother's cheeks. 'I've been working on some song lyrics,' he mumbled. '*Private* ones. I realised they were gone while we were still at school, but I thought maybe I'd left them here, so . . .'

'Don't you have them on your computer?' Justin asked.

Daniel didn't avert his gaze from the mess on the floor. 'I do, but that's not the point . . .' Then his head jerked up. 'Wait a minute. I remember now. I had them out at school . . . in English class!

I was trying to figure out if I could rhyme 'heart' with 'dark' in the middle eight.'

'You lost me at "rhyme",' Justin joked.

'Doesn't matter,' said Daniel. 'The lyrics must still be there!'

'So?' Justin shook his head as he knelt down beside his brother, starting to look through the piles of scattered papers. 'What's wrong with that? It's not like you have anything to be embarrassed about. You're a good songwriter, so . . . *oh!*' His mouth dropped open as he figured it out. 'Wait a minute. Was the song about –'

'Don't say it!' Daniel said. His eyes looked wild.

It was definitely about Debi! Justin realised. He forced himself not to let out the snort of amusement that was building inside. He was a good brother: he'd wait until after Daniel was safely gone before he gave in and guffawed.

Biting back his grin, he said, 'Look, I'll help you clean up here, and I'm sure you'll find the song at school tomorrow. I'm sure there was nothing . . . *identifiable* . . . about it, right?'

Daniel's expression looked anguished. He let out a groan.

Uh-oh. So it's totally identifiable. Justin bit the inside of his cheek. 'But these lyrics only matter because you were going to use them for your big, important Homecoming audition, right?' He blinked at his brother, trying to look innocent. 'Because we all know how much you lo-o-ove . . . Homecoming!'

The door opened before Daniel could answer – which was probably a good thing, because Justin had a feeling that his twin might just have launched himself at him at any moment.

'Daniel!' Dad bounded into the room, his hair rumpled and his face glowing with excitement.

As he came to a stop in the middle of the chaos, he didn't even *glance* at the mess covering the floor. 'Ready to get howling?'

Daniel just groaned and laid his head on his hands.

'Come on, kiddo!' Dad aimed a playful punch at his shoulder. 'Up and at 'em! Time to show all those wolves just what you're made of!'

'OK, Dad.' Daniel heaved a sigh. 'If I have to.'

As Justin watched, trying not to look amused, Daniel dragged himself out of the room like a prisoner on his way to his last meal, while their father growled and punched the air with excitement.

'Have fun!' Justin said. He waved them off cheerfully.

His twin might be a werewolf . . . but he looked more *hangdog* than Lupine tonight!

Poor Daniel, Justin thought. He shook his

head as he went back to sorting out the piles of clothes and papers on the floor. Personally, Justin couldn't think of anything that sounded more fun than a werewolf gathering. It was just too bad his werewolf brother didn't feel the same way.

Wait a minute! Justin came to a sudden stop. He stared at the band shirt he held in one hand and the pad of sheet music he held in the other. *OK, this is just plain wrong.*

How had he ended up being left alone to tidy up Daniel's room?

How did I ever end up here? Daniel wondered. *I think I'd prefer to be tidying up my messy bedroom.*

As darkness fell, the whole werewolf community of Pine Wood gathered around a group of small fires in the middle of a forest clearing. The smokiness of the burning logs mingled with the tangy smell of the pine trees that stretched high around them . . . and the musky, wild scent of about two dozen werewolves getting more and more excited.

Daniel could feel an itch of the same excitement starting in his veins . . . but more than that, he felt sheer disbelief. This was *so* not his scene! No one was wearing black. Everyone was dressed in loose-fitting, athletic clothing, ready for a quick transformation at any point. He didn't even know anyone around him except . . .

'There you are!' Kyle came swerving out of the darkness, followed by the rest of the Beasts from the football team. Firelight flickered across their faces, casting shadows across their feral grins. 'Come on, Packer! Are you ready to *run*?'

Next to Daniel, his dad laughed. 'It's like they think you're —'

'Oh, I'm ready,' Daniel said, speaking over his father to make sure he didn't reveal the secret he did not know he was keeping. He stepped hard on his dad's foot as he finished, 'I just hope I don't wear myself out here and forget myself on the football field!'

'Football field?' Dad repeated. It came out as a squeak.

'I just need to talk to my dad about something first. OK?' Daniel said to Kyle. 'Don't get started with all that *really fun* running without me, OK?'

'Not waiting.' Kyle shrugged. 'You'll have to work hard if you want to catch up with us!'

Hooting and hollering, the Beasts turned and pounded off into the darkness.

It seemed to take forever before they were finally out of earshot – which, for a werewolf, was pretty far. While Daniel waited, he watched his dad's expression shift from confusion to shock – and outrage.

'Let me get this straight,' Dad said, when it was finally safe to speak. He lowered his voice to a whisper, but it sounded as loud as thunder in Daniel's ears. 'Are you actually *pretending* to be Justin?'

Daniel grimaced. 'It's not for me, Dad, it's for him. All the guys on the team think he's a werewolf. That's why they've accepted him. If they ever find out he isn't . . .' He winced, thinking of the Beasts. 'That would make things really, really awkward. Seriously, it would be a bad idea.'

'Worse than lying?' Dad frowned. 'I don't like all this secret-keeping. Neither of you boys should be ashamed of who you are. There's nothing wrong with being a werewolf. And there's nothing wrong with being a human, either.'

'It's not forever,' Daniel said. 'It's just until Justin can show the rest of the team that he's so good, he deserves to be there, werewolf or not.'

'I'm not sure . . .' Dad started. Then he sighed. The crackling fires nearby sent shadows across his face, and he looked suddenly tired, as if all the excitement was draining out of him. 'This is my fault, isn't it? I'm the one who told Justin that he would be the werewolf. I let all the other wolves in town know what I expected, too. If I hadn't made that mistake . . .'

'Dad, it's OK.' Daniel forced a smile. 'It's all worked out . . . kind of. I mean, Justin made the team anyway. Pretty soon, he'll be able to tell the other guys the truth. We just have to cover for him until he's ready.'

'If you're sure . . .'

'I am,' Daniel said. 'You know he'd do the same for me.'

'That's true.' Dad's expression lightened. 'And in that case . . . you have some running to do,

83

don't you?' He then turned and cupped a hand to his mouth, calling in a voice that was half-shout, half-howl: 'Hey, Kyle, wait for Justin!'

Dad gave Daniel a wink.

'Great,' Daniel groaned. Taking a deep breath, he turned and jogged into the darkness, leaving the fires and the light behind.

It didn't take long to find Kyle and the other Beasts. They'd stopped by a river bank, less than a quarter mile away from the fires of the gathering. As Daniel jogged down the bank towards them, he saw Ed and Chris having a push-up competition, while Kyle played judge.

When Kyle looked up, though, he whistled for the exercise to stop. 'Hup! Twenty-nine! Thirty-three! Fifteen! Carolina!'

What?! Panicking, Daniel froze, even as he saw the others start to take up set positions. He didn't know any of the team's formations! Then

Kyle bellowed with laughter and swiped a hand through the air to stop everyone in their tracks. 'Kidding! I'm just kidding. This isn't a training session, cubs. We're here to *run*!'

The Beasts roared with excitement. All around him, Daniel could scent hair turning into fur. *It's time.*

Closing his eyes, he let the transformation happen. Waves of heat swept across him as hair sprouted across his skin, covering his face and his hands. His nails lengthened into claws, his teeth lengthened into fangs . . . and every pulse of the surrounding woods seemed to find an echo in his body.

He had *changed*.

With every one of his senses intensified, he *felt* the others begin to run even before he opened his eyes. He breathed in their excitement, the fierce rush of their competition, and felt an echoing rush in his own body. Then, he started to run.

He sprinted like lightning. He had never run so fast in his life. He hadn't even known it was possible!

'Whoa!' Ed Yancey roared his approval as Daniel raced past him. 'Go, Packer!'

With his senses on full alert, Daniel dodged and dived past trees and fallen logs, pushing himself until he and Kyle were neck-to-neck. *Do Justin proud!* he ordered himself . . .

No one could say he wasn't trying now, or wasn't doing his best to be a 'real' werewolf . . .

But seriously . . . Daniel gave a mental sigh even as he leapt over a tangle of tree roots. *Is this really all there is to it?*

OK, so when these guys turned wolf, they could all run really fast and jump really high – well, *whoopdidoo!* Could any of these knuckleheads hold a good conversation? Or write a song?

And speaking of songs . . . What *had* happened to his song lyrics? He'd definitely had them in English class – or at least, in the beginning of English class. He'd set them down to watch Justin approach Riley. But what happened to them after that?

And – *uh-oh* – what had just happened to the ground?!

Snapping out of his thoughts, Daniel looked down – and saw empty air under his feet. He had sprinted right off the edge of a cliff!

Before he could even scream on his way down, a strong, clawed hand grabbed him by the collar. Kyle hauled him up and on to solid land.

'Packer.' For once, the leader of the Beasts looked seriously impressed. 'You are one radical dude. But you're also a dumb dude. I mean, it's cool that you tried, but we all need more experience before any of us'll be ready for the daredevil thing.'

'Right,' Daniel said. He shook himself out, breathing hard. 'Oh, well. Worth a shot, right?' *Might as well pretend it was intentional!*

'Right.' Kyle grinned. 'If you were looking to become vulture-food. Now let's get back to camp.'

Daniel jogged back, his heart still hammering in his chest. He had to learn to focus – he almost ended up a werewolf-shaped splatter on the ground. As he loped along, he was surrounded by a crowd of Beasts, all of whom slapped him on the back in admiration. When they reached the group of fires, he found his dad waiting for him.

'So?' There was a funny expression on Dad's face – a mixture of hope and guilt. 'What did you think of your first real run?'

That it was pretty boring until I accidentally jumped off a cliff, Daniel thought. Then he winced. *I can't tell him that!* 'It was fun,' he said, and did his best to sound convincing.

He couldn't tell whether or not he'd succeeded. Dad only shook his head and reached out to ruffle Daniel's hair.

'You'll need to cut this soon.'

'Oh, come on!' Daniel groaned. 'I just cut it last weekend!'

'You're a wolf now, son . . . whether you like it or not.'

Dad must have seen the doubt on Daniel's face. 'You *will* enjoy this next part, though. I'm sure of it.'

'What is it?' Daniel asked.

'Just look.' Dad pointed up at the sky.

The clouds were finally beginning to part, revealing a large, white, nearly-full moon that illuminated the two dozen of Pine Wood werewolves as they pressed close together, craning their necks to gaze up at the sky. Moonlight shone down on them, bathing their faces and sending shivers up and down Daniel's body.

'What's going on?' Daniel breathed.

His dad didn't answer in words. He just put one hand on Daniel's shoulder, opened his mouth – and *howled*!

Every wolf in the gathering joined in. The sound wrapped around Daniel like a demand, pulling a response up through his body. He tipped his head back and let the howls erupt from his own throat, high and raw and true, twining around the others in the pack. Howling filled the night, eerie and melodic and hauntingly right, drawing all the werewolves together . . . and Daniel was a part of it.

Every inch of his body tingled with excitement. A wild joy swept through him, strengthening his howl. This wasn't about being macho. This wasn't about being physically strong. This was *music*, perhaps the most beautiful music he'd ever heard . . . and not only was he feeling like a real werewolf for the first time ever, but he was also suddenly getting a really good idea.

He could make *howling* a central part of his band's sound. It would give them an extra special edge, it would make them unique . . . and, even more than that, it would be a genuine tribute to a side of himself that he'd never quite understood until right now.

As Daniel gave himself up to the night and the moon, he realised: this werewolf gathering wasn't so bad after all. In fact, it was actually kind of awesome!

Chapter Four

It was forty minutes before school started when Justin stepped through the main doors the next morning. Normally, if he was up this early, he would have been yawning and complaining, but this time, he was actually early on purpose.

With less than a week until Homecoming, he was sure to find Riley here, organising . . . *something*. And no matter whether it was the Game, the Dance, or Debi's campaign, he knew he wanted to see her at work.

He was whistling cheerfully as he turned into

the first hallway – and was nearly stampeded by the Beasts as they thundered towards him.

'Packer, my man!' Kyle bellowed. His playful jostle sent Justin slamming into the lockers behind him. 'Are you ready to *run* again after school?'

'Um . . .' Justin straightened, hoping he hadn't left a dent in the lockers. He was pretty sure Kyle must be referring to last night's gathering – but what about it? All Justin's happiness at getting to school early suddenly faded away. He was a doofus for leaving so early – if he had been his usual, lazy self, at breakfast he would have been able to ask Daniel what had happened. Then he would have known what Kyle meant by 'ready to run'.

He did the only thing he could think of. He gave a shrug. 'Sure,' he said. 'Sounds like fun.'

'Yeah?' Kyle eyed him, frowning. 'You look like you could use a Pick-me-up.' He reached

93

into the pocket of his jacket and cracked open a Tupperware box. 'Here!' He held out a morsel of raw meat. 'I was saving this for lunch, but I think you need it more than I do.'

Ugh! Justin swallowed hard, backing away from the dripping red meat. *Do not gag!* he ordered himself. 'Um . . . actually, I just remembered,' he mumbled. 'I have to go help Riley with something.'

'Ha!' Ed chortled. 'First Mackenzie, now Riley! Packer, you need to make up your mind, you *player*!'

Wolf whistles chased Justin all the way down the hallway. He stuffed his hands in the pockets of his jeans and walked even faster. He didn't let himself turn around to argue, even when they started taking bets on whom Justin 'l-o-o-o-oved' more, Riley or Mackenzie . . . because he could feel that his face had turned bright red with embarrassment. The last thing he needed was to give them even more fuel for the fire!

When he finally found Riley five minutes later, he let out a sigh of relief. She had taken over an empty classroom as Base Camp for all her organising, and as early as it was, she already had three tables pushed together and covered with construction paper, markers, ribbons and notebooks. Debi, Sarah, and Eileen were all sitting at the tables, helping her make posters.

When Justin stepped inside, Riley gasped. 'Justin? What are you doing here?'

Justin shoved his hands deeper in his jeans, hunching his shoulders as all the other girls went silent, staring at him in obvious shock. Was this a *no-boys-allowed* zone, and no one had warned him? 'Um, I thought you might need a hand with all the —'

'I can't believe you're offering to help organise the Homecoming Dance! You must be the First Boy in the History of Boys to actually *volunteer*!' Riley flew around the desk and threw her arms around him. 'You're amazing!'

'Well . . .' Justin's voice came out in a near-squeak as she let go of him.

The hug had been wonderful . . . and he really liked impressing Riley . . . But he shuffled sideways, nervously. Was he really going to be the only boy here?

Then the door opened again behind him. 'Hey, Riley.' It was Daniel, giving a casual wave to the group of girls. 'Need some help?'

'I can't believe it.' Smiling, Riley hurried over to hug Daniel, too. 'The Packer twins are the best.'

Justin breathed a sigh of relief. He was not going to be the only boy after all . . .

But, he had to admit, it had been nice – a scary

kind of nice – to be 'unique' in Riley's eyes, at least for a moment.

Daniel shook his head in awe as he looked around Riley's Base Camp. Now that he and Justin had both settled into their jobs for the morning – drawing giant wolves to symbolise the football team on the banners that would hang in the auditorium – Riley was back in constant motion, like a bee that couldn't stop.

One moment, she was badgering Debi to sparkle up her T-shirt for her Homecoming Queen campaign, and the next moment she was checking drawings and inventories for the Dance. Her binder of notes looked so huge, he wouldn't be surprised if she had stayed up all night working on them.

As he watched her guzzle an energy drink, he shook his head sympathetically. Man, did she look tired.

'But Riley . . .' Debi looked apologetic as she cut another long strip of ribbon. 'I'm sorry. I really do want to help. I know how hard you're working. But I just don't know about *actively* campaigning. I mean, what if everyone just thinks I'm being pushy, or obnoxious?'

'Like Mackenzie, you mean?' Justin snorted. 'Trust me, you can't look pushy next to her.'

'This is true,' Sarah said, nodding. 'Mackenzie has the pushiness *and* the obnoxiousness covered for our whole grade.'

'And doesn't the Homecoming Queen get treated like a Queen for a whole week after Homecoming?' Daniel added. 'That means every girl in our grade would have to be part of her Court.'

'Ouch.' Eileen shuddered.

'That means that Mackenzie will have an entourage,' Riley said. 'A *school-sanctioned* entourage.' She gave Debi a stern look. 'Most girls who get voted Queen don't take advantage of it . . . but Mackenzie is *not* "most girls".'

'Do you really want to sit back and let that happen?' asked Sarah.

Debi bit her lip. 'Let me think about it.'

'Let's *all* think about it, OK?' Riley shot Daniel a playful look. 'Come on, guys. We need to *motivate* this girl!'

Her voice came out as nearly a croak, making Daniel frown. 'How's your throat doing? All those carbonated energy drinks can't be good for it.'

'I know.' She sighed as she turned back to the inventories. 'But what can I do? I need to stay awake.'

Daniel traded a concerned look with Justin.

'Well, don't forget, you *also* need to be on your game tomorrow for the Battle of the Bands audition that *you* signed us up for. So maybe you need to get some more sleep and give up the energy drinks.'

'I will be on my game tomorrow. I promise. I'm going to put *that* on . . .' Riley rummaged among her pile of papers and pulled out a crumpled sheet with line after line of scrawled instructions. Some were crossed-out, but most weren't. '. . . my To-Do List!' She made a note on what little blank space there was. Then she gathered up a massive pile of papers and clipboards and used her shoulder to shove her hair back into place. 'Now, if you'll all excuse me, I have some more organising to do.'

'For what?' Justin asked, half-rising from his seat.

'My next objective,' Riley chirped, trying and

failing to flick a rebellious strand of blonde hair out of her face.

'Which is . . .?' Daniel asked.

'Going to be taken care of,' said Riley, as Sarah helped tuck the hair behind her ear. Then her head fell forward in anguish. 'You know what? I am so busy, I'm not even sure *what* it is I'm supposed to be doing next! But I'm sure I'll find out when I get there . . .' She jostled the clipboards around until the organisation timesheet was on top. '. . . Wherever '*there*' is?'

As she hurried away, the school bell sounded, warning everyone that the first period was about to start. Daniel scooped up his books and fell into step beside Debi as they both headed towards Homeroom.

'So . . .' Debi shot him a mischievous look. 'It's a little hard to believe that *Daniel Packer* is helping to organise the Homecoming Dance – *and* auditioning to play at it, too! Aren't you going to lose street-cred with your band mates for getting so into all of this peppy stuff?'

Daniel laughed. 'Yeah, probably.' He shrugged.

Debi's curly red hair bounced around her, brushing against his shoulder as they walked beside each other. Even with the press of the crowd all around them, Daniel's werewolf senses could easily pick out the light and flowery scent of her shampoo. Better yet, the sight of her teasing grin made him feel more confident than he had since the disaster at the Meat & Greet.

'It's a little more "mainstream" than we usually like to be,' he admitted, 'but who cares? The Dance would be the biggest audience we've ever had.' *And helping to organise it means I get to spend more time with you*, he added silently.

'That's true,' Debi said. She raised her eyebrows. 'But will it "really rock"?'

Daniel winced as he recognised the phrase. 'Forget what I said at the Meat & Greet,' he said. 'Please?' *At least, forget what* Justin *said when he was pretending to be me.* 'The truth is,' he admitted, 'I wasn't thrilled when I first found out that Riley had signed us up . . . but now that I've had time to think about it, I think it's actually going to be good for us. The band needs experience in performing.'

Debi nodded understandingly as they neared their classroom door. 'So this'll be good practice.'

'Absolutely.' Daniel lowered his voice as they passed Milo lounging against his locker, typing in a text. Milo had already lost his audition; Daniel didn't want to make him feel any worse by talking about the band in front of him. 'If we can just get through the show, the guys can prove to themselves they don't have to be scared of big crowds.'

'Ha!' Milo straightened away from his locker, grinning. Obviously, he'd caught every word. 'For once, Packer, I totally agree with you.'

'Uh . . . you do?' Daniel looked at him warily.

'Absolutely,' Milo said. His grin widened into an outright smirk as he added, 'If something doesn't hurt a little bit, it's probably not worth having. Right?'

Daniel froze.

He recognised that line.

It was almost a direct quote from *No More Puppy Love*, the song whose lyrics he'd been working on yesterday in English class . . . the lyrics he had lost after Milo had 'fallen' right next to Daniel's desk!

As Daniel stared at Milo's smug expression, the truth fell into place with a sickening lurch.

He hadn't just 'lost' his lyrics. They'd been *stolen*!

'Daniel?' Debi touched his elbow, sounding worried. 'Are you OK?'

'I'm fine,' Daniel said numbly. 'It's nothing.'

But all the way into Homeroom, he couldn't stop remembering Milo's smirk. Milo definitely had Daniel's lyrics . . . but how closely had he studied them?

Daniel swallowed hard as he asked himself the real question: *How obvious is it that that song is about Debi?*

And if the answer was: *totally obvious* . . . then exactly how long would it be before Milo told everybody else at their school about it?

Chapter Five

Six hours later, Daniel was standing with his band mates outside the main auditorium. The Battle of the Bands was about to start, but he had never felt less ready. All he could think about was his stolen song, *No More Puppy Love* . . . and for once, his own band mates really weren't helping.

'I'm not sure I even *want* to win this thing,' Otto was slumped against the wall, scowling. 'We have, like, three songs that we know. Our set would last about ten minutes – maybe twelve if Daniel freestyled a solo, but that's it!'

'Yeah, man,' said Nate. 'You said you were working on new material – where is it?'

'Erm . . .' Daniel's fingers nervously drummed against his guitar. 'I did have one, but it just wasn't right. Not for Homecoming. It's too . . . intense.'

He couldn't tell his band mates what had really happened – not right before the audition. The last thing he wanted was to freak *them* out, too. But why had Milo stolen *No More Puppy Love*? And what was he planning to do with it?

Whatever his plan was, it couldn't be good. Milo had sworn a melodramatic oath to collect his vengeance, promising all of them that his 'wrath would be righteous'!

Is this the way righteous vengeance starts? Daniel wondered.

But his band mates had other things on their minds.

'"Too intense?"' Nathan shook his head

in disbelief, flicking hair the colour of army camouflage around his face. His latest colour matched his ancient, ragged camouflage coat and his khaki-painted nails. 'What are you talking about, man?' he said. 'We *are* intense. We're *In Sheep's Clothing*!'

Daniel tried to smile, but he could feel it twist into a grimace. 'Yeah, well, Homecoming is supposed to be celebratory, right? We need to play something upbeat.'

'"Upbeat?"' Nathan looked as confused as if he were hearing a foreign language. 'What does that even mean?'

Otto sagged even lower against the wall, his voice solemn. 'Whatever it is, I'm pretty sure it doesn't rock.'

'Oh, come on, guys!' Bouncing on her toes, Riley grabbed Otto's hand and pulled him upright. 'We *always* rock! And we can rock just as hard with upbeat music. We're *In Sheep's Clothing*! Let's see everyone project some positivity!'

Maybe those energy drinks are actually doing some good, Daniel thought, as he watched Riley bubble with enthusiasm. But then she started the 'warm-up exercises' and he felt his stomach sink.

'Deep breaths,' Riley commanded, 'and positive thoughts.'

Daniel eyed Nathan, who looked as confused as if he had just been asked to give the square root of 37. When Otto tried to take a deep breath, he almost choked on it.

'Um . . .' Riley's voice sounded strained. She traded a panicked look with Daniel. Then she looked back to their band mates. 'Good job, guys,' she said, with a nervous smile and a shaky thumbs-up. 'You nailed it!'

Daniel just groaned and closed his eyes. *We're doomed.*

Then a familiar, sneering voice spoke behind him. 'Good luck, guys . . . because it sure looks like you're going to need it!'

Feeling his stomach muscles tense, Daniel slowly turned around. Milo was strutting towards them, leading three other guys who were all carrying guitars. They were obviously his new band – and they all wore identical expressions of disgust.

'Is this really the "competition"?' asked the guy behind Milo. He shook his head in disgust. 'Seriously?'

'Huh.' The guy at the back smirked and strummed a jangling chord on his sleek black guitar. 'Well, this should be easy.'

The door to the auditorium swung open. Principal Caine stood just inside, her expression cool. 'Is everyone ready for the Battle of the Bands?'

Daniel forced a smile and gestured politely to Milo. 'After you guys.'

'That's right,' Milo said. 'Make way for the winners!'

Daniel put his hands in his pockets until he was sure he was not going to 'wolf-out', then followed the others inside.

With every seat empty, the auditorium looked humongous. Only Principal Caine stood inside, looking bored and impatient.

Is she really the right person to decide the music for a dance? Daniel wondered. *I doubt she's ever enjoyed a song in her life!*

Still, there wasn't any choice. Her voice echoed around the massive space as she asked, 'Who would like to go first?'

Milo and Riley both spoke at once. 'We would!'

Principal Caine sighed heavily, and glanced down at her watch as if she were only counting

111

the seconds until she could leave. 'Fine,' she said. 'We'll do a coin toss.'

'Heads!' Milo shouted. Then he punched the air, whooping, a moment later, as the coin came up. 'We win!'

'*Not yet*,' Riley muttered under her breath.

She'd said it so quietly, she probably thought that no one else had heard her, but Daniel's werewolf hearing picked it up. He traded a tight smile with her as *In Sheep's Clothing* settled down in the front seats of the auditorium, leaving Milo's band to take the stage.

It only took a minute before Daniel was leaning forward in his seat, feeling a frown on his face. Milo's group seemed to be fumbling as they plugged in their instruments, as if they hadn't done it often before – but that wasn't what was weirding him out. There was something missing. He couldn't figure out what it was, but . . .

'Hey,' Otto said, tapping Daniel on the shoulder. 'Where's their drummer?'

Milo tossed him a contemptuous look from onstage. 'We don't need a boring drummer,' he called down. 'Because unlike you guys, we're *all* rock stars in this band!' Then he grabbed the mic and swung it around, striking a pose. 'That's right . . . We are *Victor Vengeance and The Righteous Wrath!*'

Daniel had to clap one hand over his mouth to stop laughing. *Are you kidding me?*

Honestly, had Milo really taken losing out to Riley *that* badly? His band name almost exactly echoed his oath of vengeance . . . but otherwise, it made less sense than having a rock band with no drummer!

Don't laugh! Daniel ordered himself. *Do not laugh!*

Then Milo launched into their song . . . and Daniel thought he might never laugh ever again.

113

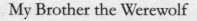

Guitars jangled. Chords broke. The tune was new and unfamiliar . . . but Daniel knew all the words.

'. . . No more puppy lo-o-o-ove!' Milo wailed.

Horror sank like a stone through Daniel's chest. *I can't believe this is happening!*

Nathan leaned over to whisper in Daniel's ear: 'Man, they need to fire whoever they got to write their lyrics!'

Daniel didn't answer. He couldn't. All he could do was listen, frozen, as his work was destroyed right in front of him.

There hadn't been any melodies in Daniel's songbook, so Milo must have come up with his own. The end result was totally different from how Daniel had imagined the song . . . but was that the only reason that it sucked?

Or were the lyrics as terrible as they made them sound?

With one final clash of chords, the song came to an end . . . and was met with an awkward silence.

Daniel might have been the only one apart from Milo who knew what had just happened, but he wasn't the only one in total shock. All around him, his band mates were staring at the stage with horrified disbelief.

Obviously, none of them have heard a song that bad in a long time, Daniel thought miserably. *I can't write a song to save my tail.*

'Ahem.' Principal Caine cleared her throat. 'We all . . . I'm sure . . . 'appreciate' your efforts, Mister "Vengeance".' She cleared her throat again, looking as if she were in actual physical pain. 'Now, *In Sheep's Clothing?* It's time for us to hear you . . . if we must.'

Daniel cringed as he heard the depressed tone in her voice. Obviously, she did not expect his band to be any better than Milo's.

And she's right, he thought. *After all, I wrote Milo's song!*

Miserably, he followed the others onstage. At least Nathan and Otto seemed more cheerful now, even as Daniel's own confidence levels had sunk to rock-bottom. As they set up, Otto even tossed his drumsticks in the air.

Right, Daniel told himself sternly. He took a deep breath. *It doesn't matter how I feel right now. I have to suck it up, for the sake of the band!*

Forcing himself to square his shoulders, he counted off. 'And a one and a two and a –!'

Otto hit the drums, and the band rocked out to the strains of *Moonlight Girl.* A song they were now pretty familiar with playing.

If Daniel had not seen Riley that morning, he would never have guessed how little sleep she'd had. Her voice soared above the band, strong and confident, as she raced up and down the stage with all the energy of an out-of-control car . . .

Hey! Daniel thought. *That's actually a good line.* It was exactly how he felt about Debi. *I should write that down later!*

For now, though, he had to focus – and, inspired by Riley and their band mates, he finally managed to shake off all the panic and misery of the last few hours.

So what if he'd messed up one song? He'd written *Moonlight Girl*, too, and that really did rock – just like his band! As they all launched into the final chorus, real satisfaction coursed through Daniel's body, making him feel like he could leap right across the empty auditorium.

He flung back his head and howled with satisfaction as the song came to a close. *If there was a real audience, they would totally be cheering!*

Unfortunately, their only audience right then

was Principal Caine . . . and she looked just as unimpressed as ever.

'Well,' she said, 'thank goodness that's finished.'

Uh-oh.

Daniel lowered his guitar, trading a worried look with Riley. *We can't have lost after all . . . can we?* He glanced nervously at where Milo and the rest of his band sat with their arms crossed. *She'd have to be totally tone-deaf to choose them . . .* But knowing Principal Caine, she really might be. In fact, that would explain a lot.

Gulping, he gathered at the edge of the stage with his band mates as Principal Caine stood up and brushed herself off, looking pointedly back at her watch.

'Come on!' Milo said. 'Who won? Did we win? We won, right?'

Principal Caine sighed. "All I can say is, the second band was less offensive . . . and marginally quieter."

Marginally quieter? Daniel blinked, barely stifling a snort. Of all the compliments he'd ever imagined for their band, that sure wasn't one of them!

'Most importantly, though,' said Principal Caine, 'the second band's song was better.'

Daniel bit back the urge to tell Principal Caine that he must have been having an off-day when he wrote *No More Puppy Love*. He got the feeling he would not be helping his own band to claim the terrible song their rivals sung as his own!

He barely even heard Principal Caine finish: '. . . And therefore, *In Sheep's Clothing* may play at the Dance. I suppose.'

'Woo!' Riley cheered and jumped in the air. 'I knew it!'

'Right on!' Nathan and Otto exchanged a high-five, while Riley danced around the stage, making to pull them all in to a group hug, only to stop when she noticed that they all looked like they had been asked to put on the gym socks from the lost property cupboard.

In the auditorium, Daniel saw Milo standing up and turning away . . . taking the last remnants of Daniel's excitement with him, just like he had stolen his song.

As Milo and his band stomped out of the auditorium, Daniel faced the truth: *In Sheep's Clothing* might have won . . . but his romantic song-writing skills had lost.

Big-time.

Chapter Six

As soon as Justin got home from football practice, he charged up the stairs.

'Congratulations, man!' He bounded into Daniel's room, where Daniel was sitting scribbling something at his desk. 'I heard about your big win!'

To his surprise, Daniel winced. 'Um, yeah.'

'"*Yeah?*" That's it?' Justin stared at him. 'You *won*, man! You defeated Milo's band! Is that all you can say about it?'

'*In Sheep's Clothing* did great,' Daniel said. His smile looked forced. 'It was good for the band. But I'm working on a new song now for Homecoming, so . . .' He started to turn back to his desk.

'Hang on a minute!' Justin took a deep breath.

OK, maybe his twin wasn't as revved about the band news as Justin had expected, but still . . . *When* would he get a better opportunity to ask this favour?

'Look,' he said. 'You know the full-moon gathering tonight . . .'

'Oh, no!' Daniel groaned. 'Dad didn't change his mind about that, did he?'

'Well –'

'He *has* to let you go instead of me, this time,' said Daniel. 'I've only had a few days off since the last gathering – and the Beasts are going to spend the whole time talking about football, anyway, since they think I'm you. All the talk about plays and tactics is all gibberish to me, and –'

122

Justin laughed. 'Calm down, Bro.' He struck a superhero pose, his hands on his hips and his chest puffed out. 'Justin to the rescue! The football king is in the house! – or, uh, at the gathering. Dad understands.'

'Good.' Daniel gave a sigh that sounded like relief, and picked up his pen again. 'In that case . . .'

'But I need some help,' Justin said quickly. 'Before I go, I need to know how to handle myself there. Won't they *notice* that I'm not a wolf? I mean, when the big . . . '*rrrrrraaarrrrrgggghhhh*' happens?' He formed claws with his hands, mimicking a movie werewolf.

'Don't worry.' Daniel shrugged. 'Transforming isn't mandatory. There are some wolves who choose not to.'

'And they don't get weird looks from all the others?' Justin asked sceptically.

'Nah,' Daniel said, 'everyone's pretty relaxed about it.'

'OK.' Justin nodded. 'I'll just say I'm not in the mood.'

'Yeah.' Daniel sounded distracted, and Justin could tell that his brother was already thinking about his music again. 'Anyway, a natural athlete like you should be able to keep up without transforming.' Daniel's last words came out as a mumble as he bent back over his songbook.

'That's not the part I'm worried about.' Justin sat on the corner of Daniel's desk, trying to catch his brother's attention. 'Didn't you say something about "howling" at the last gathering?'

Daniel's head shot up, and he pulled the same face Justin did whenever he fumbled a football. 'I forgot about the howling,' he said, slapping a hand to his forehead.

'Don't panic, Bro,' Justin said. 'I've got it all

worked out. How about if you recorded *yourself* howling on a loop? Then I can put my phone on speaker . . . and join in with the others!'

Daniel's mouth fell open. His eyes narrowed. A low growl built up in his throat, rumbling ominously. 'Are you kidding me?' he asked.

Uh-oh, Justin thought. He scooted off the desk, keeping a wary eye on Daniel's face. His twin had given him dark looks before, but never anything like this.

'Err . . . uhm . . .' Justin stammered, trying to figure out what he had said that had made Daniel go all Monster Boy. 'It was just a suggestion.'

'Tell me,' Daniel growled, 'that you are joking.'

'I, uhh . . .'

Daniel stood up from his desk. Justin could see that his hands were hairy now, and balled into fists. 'Are you seriously suggesting that you . . . *lip-sync?*'

'Well . . .' Justin shrugged, sticking his hands in his pockets. 'I figured –'

'I don't believe you!' Daniel stepped away from his desk, snarling. 'Have you ever listened to *anything* I've said about music?'

Justin tried a winning smile. 'About as often as you've listened to me talk about football.'

'Justin!' Daniel grabbed his own hair and tugged at it, looking desperate. 'Lip-syncing goes against my whole code as a musician! It's –'

'It's my only option!' Justin said. 'Come on, dude! I can't exactly sing live, can I? I don't care how caught up the other guys are in the howling – if Kyle sees that I'm not joining in, you *know* there'll be trouble. So unless you want to go to the gathering yourself, and work on your new song another night –'

'OK, fine. Fine!' Daniel sagged back down on to his chair. 'I'll do it . . . as long as you promise never to tell anyone else about this!'

'Your secret is safe with me, Bro.' Justin pulled his phone out of his pocket. 'Now help me pretend to be you . . . pretending to be me!'

Daniel shook his head and snatched the phone out of Justin's hands. 'I can't record myself howling here. I need to go to the bathroom!'

'Uh . . .' Justin stared at his brother. 'Why, exactly? I'm your twin – you don't have to hide anything –'

'I'm not *hiding*,' Daniel made a face at him. 'The acoustics are better in there . . . obviously!'

Justin rolled his eyes. '*Obviously.*'

As Daniel closed the bathroom door behind himself, Justin sighed and wandered over to the desk. The piece of paper Daniel had been working on had just four words written on it.

. . . *out-of-control car* . . .

Justin pursed his lips in a silent whistle. *Ohh-kay!*

127

As his brother's howls echoed through the bathroom next door, Justin shook his head. Yeah, he loved his twin . . . but occasionally, he had to admit, Daniel really did veer a little left of 'normal'.

Three hours later, Justin was walking through the woods with his dad. Firelight flickered from the clearing up ahead. The sound of yips and growls echoed in the distance.

Justin grinned, feeling adrenaline pump through his body.

Finally, I'm getting to see what all the fuss is about!

Just before they stepped into the clearing, Dad pulled Justin to a halt. Lowering his voice to a whisper, he asked: 'Are you *sure* you want to do this, son? I'll understand if you've changed your mind.'

128

'Don't worry, Dad!' Justin was so revved, he was actually jogging in place now. He just couldn't keep still! 'I've got it all covered – the running *and* the howling. Everything's cool!'

'Well, if you're sure . . .' Still, Dad looked nervous even as he let go of Justin's arm. 'I won't transform tonight, either, so we can tell the others that it was a "family" decision.'

'Thanks, Dad,' Justin said. And he meant it . . . but he couldn't wait any longer. He took off like a rocket, into the clearing full of firelight and action and excitement – and the Beasts, who were clustered in a hooting, wrestling group on the other side of the fires.

'Packer!' The Beasts all bellowed his name at once as Justin jogged towards them.

'At last!' Kyle said. He raised one hand to high-five Justin, and long, claw-like nails sparkled in the firelight. 'We've been waiting for you!'

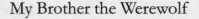

'Well, I'm here now,' Justin said, and he felt his grin widen on his face. He didn't even show the pain of the high-five, because he barely felt it. He'd been waiting all his life for this, ever since Dad had first told him, all those years ago, what it would be like to be a werewolf.

Finally, he thought. *I'm where I belong!*

'Let's run!' Kyle roared.

The Beasts all echoed his roar.

Justin launched himself forward, excitement burning through his veins.

Within moments, they were running faster than he'd ever seen before. The Beasts might be fast and strong on the football field, but they had obviously been holding themselves back until now. Justin's leg muscles seemed to scream with effort as he pushed himself to keep up, his breath coming in pants and his heart thumping crazily against his chest.

'Hey, good job keeping cool this time, Packer,' Kyle said, and whacked him on the shoulder. 'I know you're a wild man, but you'd better not run off the edge again!'

The Beasts all shouted with laughter, and Justin forced a chuckle through his burning chest. 'You know me!' he said faintly.

His head was swimming with lack of air. Maybe that was why he had no idea what they were talking about?

Or maybe 'running off the edge' is some kind of werewolf in-joke . . .?

As the Beasts slowed to a stop by a riverbank, Justin tried not to punch the air in front of them. *I did it! I kept up. And now we're having a rest . . . right?*

'Come on, now, let's run a drill for the Home-coming Game!' Kyle said. He grinned, his teeth long and feral in the darkness. 'But this time, we won't hold ourselves back – we're not in school now!'

Uh-oh, Justin thought. But as the Beasts roared and got into position, he felt the excitement come rippling back through his aching muscles.

He was here, wasn't he? And he'd kept up so far. And man . . . how many 9th graders in the world got to play football *this* hard core? If he hadn't been born into a werewolf family, he would never have even known football *got* this hard core.

By the time they all ran back into the fire-lit main clearing an hour later, Justin was streaming with sweat, his muscles felt as wrung-out as limp noodles . . . and he was happier than he had ever been.

I did it! he thought. *I survived a full-on werewolf practice!* And now . . .

Looks like it's time for . . .

'The Howling!' Kyle said. Justin spun around and saw that, in the time he had spent thinking about his relief at getting through the practice, his quarterback had transformed. His lips peeled back over his sharp teeth as he tipped his head back to face the clouds that covered the night sky. The rest of the Beasts pressed tightly around Kyle and Justin, part of the great furry mass drawing close together all around the clearing.

Time to put the plan into action, Justin thought, licking his lips nervously and shooting a quick glance at the Beasts around him. *Let's hope this works!*

The clouds pulled apart like cotton candy separating, and the moon was revealed overhead. Before Justin could even take in the sight, his body resonated with the eerie sound of high, echoing howls breaking out all around him. Every inch of skin on Justin's body prickled with primal reaction to the sound. When he looked down at his arm, he could see all the hairs standing on end.

It's show time! As surreptitiously as he could, Justin reached into the pocket of his shirt and pressed the button he'd programmed on his phone.

'*Ah-woooooooo!*' Daniel's howls projected out from his chest, high and strong and perfectly pitched. *I gotta hand it to you, Bro*, he thought with a grin, *you really do know your acoustics.*

Justin tipped back his head and opened his mouth. As 'his' howls joined all the rest, he just tried not to think of his twin shaking with outrage as he sensed the lip-syncing taking place.

After a moment, even that thought was gone, as Justin was swept up into the eerie beauty of the moment. As the wolves all around him howled in unison, his exhilaration gave way to a bittersweet thought.

I wish I didn't have to pretend.

He felt *right* here. He'd kept up with the Beasts at running, and football. He *loved* the gathering in a way that Daniel never could.

But Justin would never be a werewolf, no matter how much he wanted to be.

Forget it, he ordered himself, and tipped his head back farther. *You don't have to turn into a wolf to be awesome. Just enjoy the moment!*

And for that moment, it was genuinely perfect . . .

Until Kyle turned and gave Justin a friendly slap in the chest.

The sound of Daniel's howling switched off abruptly – to be replaced by the music of *In Sheep's Clothing*!

Kyle had hit the 'skip' button on Justin's phone!

'. . . *a smile as bright as stars . . .*'

And of all the songs to blare out into the still night . . .

'. . . *hair that shines like fire . . .*'

Every werewolf in the clearing was silent. They turned to stare at him as a group. As the music played and played, Justin scrabbled to pull out the phone from his pocket. His fingers, slick with sweat, slipped and fumbled.

Oh no, oh no, oh no!

Panic thundered through his chest. The weight of stares felt crushing as the music played on and on.

Now they'll know I've been faking it!

'Hey . . .' Ed Yancey's face broke into a grin. His long teeth glinted in the firelight. 'I like it! Turn it up, dawg.'

Justin took out the phone and the mini-speaker and turned up the volume.

'A song about the moon, man!' Chris grooved to the beat, the hair on his face rippling as he broke out into a dance. 'Right on!'

As Justin watched, sharp-toothed grins broke out across the clearing, from kids and adults alike. The werewolves were totally digging the music!

Daniel is never going to believe this, he thought. Laughing, he watched their dad lead the other adult werewolves in an unbelievably embarrassing, old-fashioned dance. *Have I started a whole new werewolf tradition?*

He let the music play on as the wolves grooved all around him. It was only when the song came to an end that he finally hit the button to turn it all off . . . and then, grinning, he waved.

The other wolves yipped and cheered their applause, and Justin saw his dad smiling across the clearing – he looked as relieved as Justin felt.

The wolves were all still laughing as they moved back to take their original places. As the sound of howling rose up again to fill the clearing, Justin slipped his phone back into his pocket. He waited until everyone's heads were safely tipped back before he put his phone back in his pocket and pushed the button to re-start Daniel's howl-loop.

Then he felt someone watching him.

He glanced up quickly. Kyle had turned away from the moon to stare at him, eyes narrowed.

Justin tipped his head back fast and dropped his hand away from his pocket as if he'd been burned.

Sorry, Bro, he thought, as he felt Kyle's suspicious gaze rest on him. He closed his eyes and threw himself into matching the timings of his brother's recorded howls. *It's time for me to get really, really good at lip-syncing . . .*

Chapter Seven

By the time the school bell rang for lunch the next day, Daniel was staggering with exhaustion. Just outside his last classroom, he stumbled to a halt next to one of Riley's campaign posters and found himself staring at it in a daze, unable to look away from the photograph of Debi in mid-cheer. Her curly red hair streamed down her back as she raised her pom-poms, laughing with delight. Big red letters above and below the picture read:

'*Vote Debi! Vote Debi! VOTE DEBI!*'

The words ran together in Daniel's bleary

gaze. *DebiDebiDebiDebiDebi* . . .

Whoa! He blinked hard, trying to snap himself awake. *How does Riley do it?* He knew for a fact that Riley must have been getting even less sleep than he had for the past several nights, yet she had somehow managed to plaster bright posters all over the school at the same time as doing all her homework *and* organising every single detail for the Homecoming Game *and* the Dance.

Daniel, on the other hand, could barely walk!

Sighing, he shook his head and started forward. But the sight of Debi's delighted grin on the poster pulled him back.

There was a *reason* he had not slept last night, and it had everything to do with her. Now that Milo had lost the Battle of the Bands, what was he going to do with the stolen lyrics? It would be bad enough just to have another band using Daniel's song. But if Milo ever went to Debi and told her that the song was about her . . .

Daniel shuddered. *Maybe he doesn't even know. How could he be sure?*

Then he looked back at the poster and sighed. *Come on. It's pretty obvious. Who else at this school is worth writing a song about?* Even a jerk like Milo had to be smart enough to figure that out. *I might as well have written Debi's name on a sheet of paper bordered by a big red heart with an arrow through it!*

Closing his eyes, he ran through the lyrics in his head . . . and cringed. How many times had he used the word 'red'? *At least three times before the end of the second verse,* he answered himself silently.

Opening his eyes again, he looked straight at the poster – and at Debi's distinctive bright red hair in her photograph. He swallowed hard.

I have to do something about this!

He turned around just as Milo walked past, staring intently at an expensive-looking smartphone. Steeling himself, Daniel followed him.

He caught up with the other boy at Milo's locker. 'Hey.'

Milo blinked, lowering his phone. 'Packer?' Then his lip curled into a sneer. He tossed the phone into his open locker, which was plastered with promo stickers for his new band – and drawing after drawing of Milo himself in rockstar poses, surrounded by adoring crowds, holding up signs saying '*Victor Venjeance*'. Daniel hoped the misspelling was intentional.

'What do *you* want?' Milo asked.

Daniel gritted his teeth and leaned closer. The hallway was too crowded to take any chances, and he couldn't afford for anyone else to hear what he was about to say. 'I want to know,' he said quietly, 'what you're planning to do with what you've got.'

'Excuse me?' Milo widened his eyes. 'I have

no idea what you're talking about . . . unless you mean my rocking new band? I'm afraid we're not hiring.' He shook his head in pity. 'Sorry, Packer. You just don't "fit the band".'

That sounded like what Daniel had said when he told Milo he couldn't be in *In Sheep's Clothing*.

'That's not . . .' Daniel began. Then he saw Milo's lips twitch.

Oh, yeah. He knows exactly what I'm talking about. This is his idea of being 'funny'!

Hot anger flashed in Daniel's chest, and a wave of itchiness prickled across his arms. *Don't let me change now!* He took a deep breath, trying to shove his emotions down. 'Milo, I *know* you took my lyrics. I want them back!'

'Oh, that?' Milo smirked. 'Are you sure you actually want to claim credit for *those* lyrics, Packer?'

The itchy prickle on Daniel's arms was

shifting into a burn. He ignored the pain, but he couldn't stop the itching feeling as it spread across his scalp. He could actually feel the hair on his head growing now. Could *Milo* see it happening?

Just walk away, son. That was what Dad would have told him . . . and he knew it would have been the right thing to do. But he couldn't – not while Milo was standing there smirking at him. As long as Milo kept those lyrics, he could show them to Debi at *any* time.

'Just give them back,' Daniel growled, his gums beginning to itch. 'Now!'

Milo snorted. 'Why do you even care? We both know that they suck.'

Oh, yeah? Then why did you use them for your big audition? Daniel wanted to snarl the question like an accusation. But he didn't dare. The transformation had begun. If he opened his mouth now, Milo would see long, sharp wolf-teeth, fully revealed.

'Ha!' Milo grinned triumphantly. Turning to beckon in the passers-by, he raised his voice. 'Look at this – the great Daniel Packer *finally* has nothing to say . . . because he knows I'm right – he *is* a terrible songwriter!'

'*Grrrrrrr!*' The growl that emerged through Daniel's closed lips was so deep and feral, Milo flinched. A ripple of shock ran through the watching crowd, which was getting larger and larger.

Just great. I still don't have the lyrics . . . and if I don't get out of here fast, everyone will see me go 'furry'!

Daniel swung around, physically shaking with frustration. He stormed off down the hall without looking back. Still, he could hear the excited whispers that erupted behind him.

He couldn't turn and talk his way out of this,

because his mouth was having trouble containing his fangs. He couldn't even give a dismissive, 'he's talking nonsense' wave, because his hands were covered in thick fur.

When he saw a darkened, empty classroom to his left, he lunged inside, quickly closing the door behind him. Then he hurried around the room, pulling down the blinds to cover all the windows. It was only when the whole room was a safe pitch-black that he finally let himself collapse on to the floor in the far corner, wrapping his arms around his legs and opening his mouth before his teeth burst through his whole face. Closing his eyes, he took a long, deep breath, the way his dad had shown him.

Just calm down and the changes will go away. Just calm down . . .

The door opened. A slanted shaft of light fell across the floor, stopping just at the edge of his sneakers. If it opened just a few inches more, that light would reveal a freaky fur-boy sat in the corner, feeling sorry for himself. Daniel started to move to his left, thinking he could hide in a cupboard, when . . .

'Daniel?'

It was Debi. Daniel could see her, but she couldn't see him. She stood in the doorway, peering into the darkness. 'Are you in here?' She lifted one hand, reaching for the light switch.

'Don't!' Daniel rasped. His words were muffled by his long, sharp teeth. Fur prickled along his arms. His hair brushed against his shoulders, a full three inches longer than it had been only ten minutes ago. He held himself frozen still.

Debi dropped her hand to her side and shut the door behind her, closing them both in full darkness. 'It's OK.' Her voice was low and sweet. 'We all cry sometimes.'

What?! Daniel's mouth dropped open in outrage. He scrambled to his feet. *I am NOT crying!* 'I –'

But he slammed his mouth shut as his brain caught up with him. *What else is she supposed to think? I can't exactly tell her, 'It's OK, I'm just turning into a werewolf!'*

'Right,' he finally mumbled. His fingers curled into painful fists, his claws pricking into his palms as he mumbled, 'Thank you . . . for understanding.'

'I don't just understand. I'm *impressed*.' Debi moved gracefully through the darkness but stopped several feet away from him, a shadow in the dark. Her voice was gentle. 'You did the right thing, walking away from that argument. Most boys I know would have argued back and made more trouble.' She sighed, and the air stirred softly between them. 'I think it's braver to walk away. It means you're a really strong person.'

'Um . . .' Daniel coughed uncomfortably. 'I don't know about that.'

The truth was, if he hadn't had to escape before the transformation was complete, he *definitely* would have had a full-on argument with Milo. Then Debi wouldn't have been anywhere near as impressed with him. *I never thought there could be an upside to my werewolfness being out of control!*

'Everyone could tell that Milo was acting like a jerk,' Debi said. 'The fact that you left instead of staying to yell back at him . . . that means that you were willing to be the bigger person.' Her voice dropped to a whisper. 'I . . . really like that about you.'

It was a relief that the darkness was hiding the stupid grin he knew was on his face . . . because if Debi saw it, she would know *exactly* how he felt.

And yet, at the same time, he hated that the

darkness was hiding his stupid grin. If Debi saw it, she would know *exactly* how he felt – and then, maybe, he'd finally find out how *she* felt, too.

But then, if that wasn't the way he hoped . . .

Argh! He almost groaned. How could he feel so much relief and heartache at the same time? Was this even normal? And why did it always seem so . . . *vital* that the girl he liked never actually found out that he liked her?

'Daniel?' Debi said. 'You're being really quiet. Are you sure you're OK?'

If he spoke now, with his emotions this torn, it would definitely come out as a growl. Daniel closed his mouth . . . but the sound that came out was a high-pitched, puppy-like whine that made him cringe with embarrassment.

It was even worse than growling.

'Oh, *Daniel!*' Debi let out a soft cry of sympathy. 'You're still crying! You poor thing!'

What? No! Daniel cleared his throat, desperately trying to find a way to speak.

She raced through the darkened room and flung her arms around him before he could say a word.

Oh, no! She's going to figure it all out! Even as Daniel soaked in the feeling of her arms around him, he tensed up. *She's going to feel my long hair . . . and smell the stench of* wolf *. . . and then she's going to run away, because she'll know that I'm a big* freak!

Wait a minute. She's not running.

In fact, she was nestling against him in the sweetest, best hug of his life.

I can't believe this!

Slowly, cautiously, Daniel lifted his arms . . . and hugged her back.

Debi's hair brushed against his cheek, smelling of summer. Her arms were warm around his back. He tipped down his head to rest it against her hair. Closing his eyes, he took a long, deep breath. His wolf-senses open made the sensation seem impossibly perfect, but he had a feeling it would have been even if he was just a regular boy.

All of a sudden, he did not know why he had such trouble talking to her in the hallways, or in the front yards of their homes. Talking to Debi just felt . . .

Absolutely perfect, he thought.

'So . . .' Debi finally stepped back a full minute later. She let out a breathy laugh, sounding suddenly shy. 'I, um . . . I'll see you in Spanish, then?'

'Right.' Daniel stuck his hands in his jeans pockets, nodding even though he knew she couldn't see him. He rocked back and forth on his heels, feeling off-balance. 'See you there. I just need a minute first to . . . uh . . .'

'Don't worry.' Debi put her hand on his arm

in a quick, reassuring touch. 'I understand. And I promise, you have *nothing* to be embarrassed about.'

Her soft footsteps hurried across the room. The door opened and closed behind her.

Daniel took a deep breath, replaying the hug in his mind, even though he had not been able to see anything the entire time. Running his tongue over his teeth, he found them just the same size as normal – not sharp, or 'fang-y' at all.

Have I been de-werewolfed by Debi?

He turned on the light a moment later, and let out a relieved sigh. His arms and hands were completely fur-free. Being with Debi was so nice, so relaxing, that it made him human again. All he still had to do was a quick fix-up of his hair and nails, and he would be officially back to normal.

Well . . . He rolled his eyes at himself even as he knelt down to dig through his backpack for

153

the scissors he always carried with him nowadays to cut his wolf-lengthened nails and hair.

At least I'll be back to my *version of normal.*

Chapter Eight

By the time school ended for the day, Justin was itching to find Riley. She was hard to catch up with these days — as the countdown to Homecoming started, she could be almost anywhere in the whole school. Even the world. Luckily, he'd figured out a perfect strategy to track her down.

He moved along the hallways with a mission: *See this school the way Riley would!* Which corners were missing posters for Debi's campaign? Which hallways weren't bannered enough yet for the Homecoming Game? He narrowed his eyes as he turned a corner. If he could just figure out where she was headed next . . .

'Ahhh!' He collided straight into somebody. 'Sorry!' He flung out his hands to catch his victim, wincing when he noticed *who* it was.

Beaming, Mackenzie Barton clutched his hands and gracefully pirouetted right into Justin's arms. 'You see?' She gestured sweepingly to the other students lingering in the hallway, drawing them all in to watch. 'Look how well I dance. And even Justin . . .' She raised her eyebrows as she gestured to him. '. . . Well, he's hardly even clumsy, is he? As boys go, anyway.'

There was a smattering of catcalls, and Justin felt his cheeks heat up. 'I don't know about that,' he mumbled, ducking his head. 'Mackenzie, I'm just –'

She spoke over him, aiming her words straight at the others. 'Why, we make a pretty good team – wouldn't you agree, Justin?'

Oh, no. With a jolt of horror, Justin finally realised what she was doing: campaigning for Homecoming Queen! *And I've played right into her hands.*

Unfortunately, she was still waiting expectantly for his response, and so was everyone else in the crowd. Justin opened his mouth to speak – then gave up. There was nothing safe to say in this situation.

'Mmm,' he mumbled, and smiled vaguely as he skirted around her, aiming to escape.

Mackenzie caught his hand just as he passed her. 'Just check this out!' Her legs kicked out, her skirt whirled, and she did a fabulously twirly, dance-y move that sent her spinning right into his arms . . . as if they'd carefully choreographed it . . . *together*!

'You see?' she announced to the crowd, tipping

back her head and grinning. 'What a partnership!'

This time, the applause was enthusiastic.

'Woo!'

'Go Mackenzie!'

'Cute couple,' someone called out from the back.

Justin gritted his teeth and winced as a whole group of girls converged on Mackenzie admiringly, while the rest hung back to give him speculative looks.

'Justin!' Detaching herself from her admirers, Mackenzie hurried after him down the hall, her voice sharp and commanding. 'Don't run away! You need to get behind this now.' As she caught up with him, she grabbed his shirt-sleeve to pull him to a stop. 'The Mackenzie Express is going non-stop to Queendom. Don't you want to be on a winning team?'

'Oh, for . . .!' Groaning, Justin turned to face her. 'Mackenzie, what does it *matter* what I think? What makes you think I'm going to be Homecoming King?'

Mackenzie smiled at him with all her teeth showing. 'It's the word on the street, Justin. And trust me – I am *very* good at figuring out what the little people like.'

"*The little people?*" Justin shook his head in disgust. 'Well, we're not *on* a street. We're in a school hallway, and I'm –'

'Whatever.' Mackenzie waved off his protest. 'The point is, that's the goss. You have the vote!' Her smile hardened. 'And you're going to take me with you.'

Justin set his teeth together. 'Even if you're right about me –'

'Oh, I am.' Mackenzie finally dropped her smile, as she crossed her arms to study him like a science experiment. 'Trust me, I don't understand it either. But . . .' She shrugged. 'I suppose there is something "underdog" about you.'

You don't know how right you are, Justin thought glumly.

'So . . .' Mackenzie gave him a triumphant smile. 'When are we going to start practising our dance for tomorrow night?'

'What?!' Justin barely held back a groan. *Where is Riley when I need her?* He twisted to look over his shoulder, hoping desperately to see a flash of blonde hair, posters and clipboards. Unfortunately, Riley was nowhere to be seen . . .

. . . But Kyle was. *Phew.* 'Sorry.' Justin faked a smile as he backed away from Mackenzie, nodding towards the group of Beasts who were moving in a rowdy pack down the other end of the hallway. 'I'm pretty busy with football practice right now. So . . .' He shrugged, holding up his hands. 'I won't be able to squeeze in any dance practice.'

'*You* –!' Mackenzie's eyes flashed almost demonically. She seemed to catch herself just in time, cutting off whatever nastiness had been about to spill out of her mouth. Instead, her lips curved back into a false smile and her voice turned sugary-sweet. 'No biggie.'

Her hand snaked out and grabbed his arm before he could escape. She leaned closer, her voice turning breathy. 'I've seen you play running back, remember? I know you have good footwork. I'm sure you can improvise at the Dance tomorrow night.'

'Uh . . .' Justin tried to pull his arm free as subtly as he could.

Her eyebrows lowered into a frown. 'Honestly, it wouldn't be so bad if that silly girl, Riley, wasn't being so *secretive* about the music that's going to be played at the Dance. How am I supposed to prepare if she insists on being so irritating about it?'

'*What did you just say?*' For the first time since their conversation had begun, Justin stopped trying to back away. Instead, he stepped closer. 'Do *not* talk about Riley like that!'

'OK, OK.' Mackenzie flapped a hand at him in dismissal. 'I'll see you later, partner. Right now, I have a dress to try on!'

'Grrrrr . . .'

Anger burned like fire in Justin's chest as he watched Mackenzie stride away. The growl that rumbled through his chest was as feral as any he'd ever heard from Daniel. He had to force himself not to chase after her, just to explain exactly how wrong she was – about *everything*.

Forget her, he ordered himself. *Riley's going to make sure that Debi wins. That'll show Mackenzie exactly what the "little people" think of her.*

He swung around – and found Kyle standing *right there*, less than half a foot behind him!

Sometimes, he really hated werewolf super-speed.

Sighing, he reached up one hand for the stinging high-five. 'What's up, dude?'

'What's up with *me*?' Kyle raised his eyebrows. For once, there was no smile on his face. 'The question is, Packer . . . what's up with *you*?'

As the leader of the Beasts studied him through narrowed eyes, Justin had to force himself not to squirm. He felt like he was being held under a magnifying glass. Yet again, he cursed himself for his mistake at the gathering last night. Why hadn't he been more careful with his phone? If Kyle figured out that Justin had been lying the whole time about being a werewolf . . .

'I'm fine,' he said heartily. 'Totally fine! In fact, I'm *lu*-fine . . .' He tried not to wince as he thought about just how dumb a word 'lu-fine' was.

'Oh, yeah?' One corner of Kyle's mouth

twitched upwards. 'And you're really ready for the game tomorrow?'

'Dude, I was *born* ready,' Justin said . . . and wondered how he could stop talking in clichés and made-up words.

It seemed to have worked, though. Kyle gave him a toothy grin. 'Well, if Mackenzie's there as a cheerleader, and she makes you *growl* like you did just now . . .' He clapped Justin on the back. 'The other team won't stand a chance!'

The rest of the Beasts crowded around them, bellowing with laughter, and Justin's mouth dropped open.

'Wait a minute,' he said. 'I'm not . . . I mean, Mackenzie isn't . . .'

Chris Jackson shook his head at him. 'Try a new one, Packer! We've all seen how much time you've spent with her lately.'

'That's just . . . that's . . . oh, forget it!' Justin

cut himself off, groaning silently.

If he told them he didn't have a thing for Mackenzie, they'd just go back to teasing him about Riley. That would be worse. *There's no point giving them any more ammo!*

Anyway, what he really wanted was just to *get* to Riley, as soon as possible. 'Look,' he said. 'It's great to see you guys, but –'

'Packer's right,' Kyle said. 'That's enough about his love life! The gym's empty right now, so we should run some quick drills, make sure we're sharp enough for the game tomorrow. Come on!'

The Beasts roared their readiness and stampeded off in a group, their thundering footsteps echoing through the halls. Giving up, Justin let the group sweep him along towards the gym.

He would have to find Riley a little later, and hope that he was not too late.

It was a full hour before the Beasts were finally ready to head home. By then, Justin had to use all his energy just to stand upright at the top of the school steps, weathering a set of farewell high-fives that threatened to send his aching, wrung-out body crashing to the cement.

The moment that he saw the last Beast disappear around the corner, Justin let himself slump, breath whistling out of him. He turned to head back inside the school, almost moaning with relief. Finally – finally! – he could find Riley and spend some time helping her out.

At least, that was the plan. Unfortunately, his legs refused to obey orders. When he tried to turn, they stayed stubbornly rooted to the ground. His upper body twisted . . . but his legs didn't. Hopelessly off-balance, he started to fall.

He grabbed hold of the wall just in time

to keep from plastering himself all over the cement steps.

At least the Beasts didn't see this! He'd managed to keep up with them all through the drills, no matter what the cost in pain. But now that the drills were over, his body was refusing to play along with the pretence.

Ignoring the snickering from Milo and his friends as they passed him on their way out, Justin hobbled into the school building. He had to hang on to the wall with every step.

Too bad Mackenzie Barton isn't here to see me now, he thought, and shook his head ruefully. *If she saw me moving like this, no way would she stay on my case about that dumb, stupid dance!*

It seemed to take forever as he shuffled along the hallways, but he finally found Riley in an empty classroom, her head propped on one hand and her long blonde hair trailing in a smooth wave over her face and across a stack of papers on her desk. She didn't look up when he hobbled into the room.

Good. Justin paused a moment to straighten his shoulders, forcing himself to rise up out of his half-crouched pose. *Come on, muscles. Just give me two more minutes of dignity so I don't look like an idiot in front of her!*

He started forward, trying for a normal walk. His legs and back felt like they were screeching in protest, but he locked a smile on his face. 'So, Riley, it looks like –'

'Aaah!' Riley jerked, her arms flailing. Papers flew through the air, scattering across the floor. 'I'm not asleep! I wasn't sleeping! I'm just – oh, nooo!' She let out a moan of frustration as she looked up at the clock on the wall. 'I *totally* fell asleep! I can't believe I let myself fall asleep when there's so much *work* to do!'

'Come on, Riley . . .' Justin rolled his eyes as he walked towards her. 'You've been working too much, you've barely slept for the whole past week. I don't think the Homecoming Police are going to arrest you for taking a five-minute power-nap.'

'I don't know. I think the Homecoming Police are pretty strict about that kind of thing.' Half-laughing, Riley combed back her hair and dropped down to her knees to start gathering up the scattered papers. 'Seriously, though, I can't afford to lose any more time, not even five minutes. There's only one day left!'

'Then it's a good thing I'm here to help. See?' Justin started to lower himself down to a crouch, to help scoop up papers from underneath the desks.

It was the last straw for his aching legs. They gave out completely, sending him crashing towards the ground. 'Aaah!'

'Justin!' Dropping the papers she'd already gathered, Riley lunged forward to try to catch him.

I cannot fall on top of Riley! With one last desperate burst of energy, Justin yanked his upper body backwards even as she grabbed his shirt . . .

. . . And the sound of tearing cloth filled the air.

Justin landed on his butt with a thump. Cool air filtered on to his chest through the rip in his shirt. A few feet away, Riley blinked at him from where she'd flopped amid a massive mess of scattered papers.

Some hero I am! Justin thought.

There was a moment of silence as they stared at each other. Then they both burst out laughing.

'So,' he said, and pulled out a piece of paper

from under his legs. 'Bet you're glad I'm here to help, huh?'

Riley shook her head, giggling. Her usually smooth hair was mussed, her preppy buttoned-up blouse was wrinkled, and Justin thought she'd never looked more adorable. 'You know what?' she said. 'Maybe you're right. Homecoming or not . . . we *both* really need to get some rest!'

Daniel shook his head as he carried even more supplies into Justin's bedroom that night. This time, his twin had asked for a glass of water, a bag of ice cubes, and a bag of frozen peas from the freezer.

'Bro, are you sure this is a real medical treatment?' Daniel asked. He set the peas on Justin's bedside table and raised his eyebrows as he passed Justin the ice cubes. 'I have to say, this is the weirdest thing I've ever seen you do, even for football – and that's saying something!'

'Trust me,' Justin said. 'I'm ready to try anything right now. Whatever works to stop the pain!' He pushed himself up on his bed with obvious effort and rolled up the legs of his sweatpants. When the bag of ice cubes touched his bare skin, he let out a moan.

'All this from a practice session?' Daniel said. 'Glad I'm not a werewolf.' Before Justin could say a word, Daniel winced with realisation. 'Right, right . . . I just forgot for a minute.' He sighed and picked up the football that sat on Justin's desk. It was no wonder that he got confused sometimes – Justin was just so obviously *better* at the whole werewolf lifestyle than he was! Daniel grimaced as he thought back to the other guys at the first werewolf gathering. They'd all focused so hard on strength and sports. It was definitely better that Justin had gone to the second gathering in his place.

But then . . . what did that say about Daniel?

Like it or not, he had to spend the rest of his life as a werewolf. When was *he* going to find a way to fit in with the others?

OK, no more thinking about that. There's no point.

Looking to distract himself, Daniel pointed at the provisions Justin had asked for. 'Aren't those cold? That really looks like it should hurt.'

'No way.' Justin finished packing the peas and ice around his legs. 'That last practice is what hurt me – *this* is some sweet relief. I have to be back on my game by tomorrow, otherwise Kyle will get *really* suspicious.' He shuddered, and this time, Daniel didn't think it was because of the ice cubes. 'You should have seen the look on his face when my phone started blaring that song of yours.'

173

Daniel snorted. 'Did it look like this?' He stretched his own face into a blatantly unimpressed expression.

Justin laughed. 'Yeah, kind of.'

'Then he was probably just reacting to the song,' Daniel said firmly. He dropped down on to the chair near Justin's bed, absently tossing the football from hand to hand.

'What's up, dude?' Justin asked as he rearranged the ice packs.

'Nothing,' said Daniel, though he could hear how lame that sounded. He went for casual: 'I suppose everyone else had a similar look, huh?'

'Are you kidding?' Justin said, shaking his head. 'All the other werewolves really dug that song. At one point, I thought they would form their own mosh pit.'

'*Really?*' Daniel asked, trying to be cool, but suspecting he was failing.

'Yeah, Daniel,' said Justin. 'That song rocked . . . You know, for a sappy ballad about Deb . . . uh, *some girl* that some guy really likes. The Puppy something or other.'

Daniel allowed himself a dumb grin, just for a moment – well, it was nice to know not everyone thought his music sucked. Did they really like it, or was Justin being polite?

Daniel focused on the football in his hands. 'Are you ready for the game tomorrow?'

On the bed, Justin aimed a narrow-eyed glare at him from mid-stretch. 'Dude. Do I *look* ready?'

'Right. Sorry, sorry.' Daniel bounced the football nervously in his hands. 'I'd stand in for you again if I could, but . . .'

'I get it,' Justin said. 'You've got a gig.' His words were muffled by his blankets as he wriggled underneath them.

'That's right.' Daniel couldn't help it – he felt

a stupid grin stretch across his face at the words. 'I have a gig! An actual gig . . . The first time I ever played a note, I could hear the roar of a crowd . . .'

Justin grinned at him. 'You sure that wasn't just the roar of the neighbours, telling you to keep it down?'

'Ouch,' Daniel said, mock-wincing as he put the football back on Justin's desk. 'Hey, are you *sure* you'll be OK to play tomorrow?'

'Oh, believe me . . .' Justin gritted his teeth as he readjusted the ice packs yet again. 'I'm going to show those Beasts I'm as tough as any of them, werewolf or not. I'll just rest up my muscles tonight and be fighting fit for the game tomorrow.'

'Rock on, dude.' Daniel gave his twin an encouraging fist bump. 'Now I'd better go work on my own prep.'

His head was already back in the music zone as he hurried through their shared bathroom to his own bedroom, where his desk was covered with lyric and music sheets – and a single sheet of paper covered with possible song titles. *That* was what Daniel was aiming for now: his band's set-list for the gig tomorrow.

Tonight he had to make the final decision on which songs to include. *In Sheep's Clothing* had just five songs to make an impression – and to make the band's first real gig a success! Every single song had to be memorable.

But which ones were the *best*?

As Daniel sat down at the desk, a doodle at the bottom of the page caught his eye.

'*No More Puppy Love – ??????*'

No way! Daniel cringed. What had he been thinking? Not only had Milo stolen the song, he'd completely ruined it with that misguided cover version. How could Daniel ever believe in it again after hearing it suck so badly? Plus, *In Sheep's Clothing* hadn't even had a chance to rehearse it!

And that's not even the worst part, Daniel realised. No, the worst part was: if they played it at the Homecoming Dance, then Debi would hear it – and she would know he had written it about her.

How could she not? He shook his head at his own idiocy. All those references to red hair. But maybe, if she *just happened* to change her hair colour between now and tomorrow . . . But he didn't want her to do that.

She's perfect just as she is, Daniel thought dreamily. He started doodling more words in the corner of the page. *'Red like flame . . . red like an exploding star . . . red like a heart on fire . . .'*

Stop! Danger! He tossed down the pencil with a shudder. *That's exactly how I got into trouble last time!*

No More Puppy Love was full of telltale

phrases just like those. If Debi heard him sing it tomorrow night, she would know without a doubt – as would everyone else at the dance! – that Daniel was crushing on her.

Awkward!

Worse still, if the band played it during the Homecoming King and Queen's ceremonial dance, then Daniel could find himself singing a song that was blatantly about Debi *while she was dancing with another boy!*

The thought made him gulp with horror.

Not. Going. To. Happen!

No More Puppy Love was definitely a dead song . . . at least for now. He just couldn't take the risk.

Quickly, he scribbled in the last song on the playlist – *Barbed Wire on Fire* – a song that rocked *safely*, without giving away anything embarrassing. Just as he was packing his lyric and music sheets

179

away, he heard his mom call up from the bottom of the stairs:

'Boys? I could have sworn I had a whole bag of peas in the freezer. Have either of you seen it?'

Uh-oh. Daniel snickered, thinking of Justin's "medical treatment". He decided to let Justin answer that question. And thank him later for saving dinner . . .

I hate peas!

Chapter Nine

Well before half-time in the Homecoming Game, Justin was already feeling good. His muscles might still be aching, but they had not let him down. Yet.

Maybe he wasn't completely back to top speed, but hey – with Pine Wood comfortably ahead, he didn't have to be! With the game going so well, he could take it easy. His legs would carry him through just fine, as long as he didn't push himself too hard.

Unless Mackenzie keeps on cheering for me! Justin cringed, feeling his focus waver as Mackenzie's voice rose above the noise of the crowd, aimed straight at him . . . *again*! As captain of the cheerleading squad, she hadn't cheered a single cheer at any other player today.

'Packer, Packer, you're no fool! On this field, you so rule!'

Justin's shoulders hunched. He tried not to look at any of the other players on his team. He was too afraid of what their expressions might be. *At least Daniel isn't here.* Justin could just imagine what his twin would say about Mackenzie's 'lyrics'!

Even though Daniel was off preparing for the gig, Justin knew Riley was here sitting in the bleachers, listening to those cheers along with the rest of the school. Could Mackenzie make it any clearer to everyone in hearing range that she considered Justin her new 'interest'? And could she possibly think of a *worse* way to embarrass him in front of the rest of his team?

When Kyle called a huddle, Justin let out a sigh of relief. There was no way he could concentrate on the game right now with Mackenzie staking her personal claim on him in front of Riley and everyone else. It was nothing but a pleasure to huddle safely among the rest of the Beasts . . . at least, until Kyle gave him a hard glare.

'It's time for you to stop showing off for your girlfriends, Packer!'

Justin stared at him. 'I'm not –'

'Save it,' Kyle snapped. 'Maybe you're busy enjoying all that cheering, but Mackenzie Barton isn't in charge here. *I* am. I need you back in the game, and I need you to start giving it your *all*. You can deal with your love life on your own time, Packer. Just don't let it interfere with the game! If we make this play, we'll be twenty points ahead. Then we can coast for the second half. Got it?'

'Got it!' Justin could have cheered himself with relief. 'Which play are you calling?'

Kyle's fierce grin showed all his teeth. 'We're going to pull a *Rabid* Wolf!'

Oh, no.

Justin felt all his relief drain away, leaving his legs ready to sag underneath him. He had to clear his throat before he could speak again. 'Are . . . are you sure about that?'

'Am I sure?' Kyle gave Justin a disbelieving look. 'Are you seriously questioning me on this, Packer? You know how strong that play is for us.'

The Rabid Wolf play was one of the most effective they'd ever developed . . . and the single hardest play for Justin, as the team's running back, to pull off. He would have to charge straight through the line of scrimmage and sprint downfield to catch a long pass from Kyle, all at top speed, with players from the other team doing everything they could to slow him down.

Even when he was fighting fit, that play was *intense*. It took everything he had to do it right, even when everything else was going well. But with his legs still aching from yesterday . . .

Justin swallowed hard. *I don't think I can make it.*

He tried to sound casual. 'I'm just not sure we need it right now, when the game's going so well. Shouldn't we save it in case we need it later?'

'Hey, we're the *wolves*,' Chris said. 'Wolves don't play it safe!'

Kyle gave Chris a high-five. 'You've got it, dawg. And as for you, Packer . . .' He gave Justin a knowing look. 'If you make this TD, we'll be ahead the twenty points we need. After that, we'll *have* to relax so the score isn't suspiciously high.'

'Right . . .' Justin shrugged. They all knew they couldn't afford to win by too much, not if they were going to keep the werewolves' secret safe. But still . . .

'And that means . . .' Kyle paused meaningfully. 'If you make this TD, you'll be done. You can sit on the bench for the whole second half.'

Yes! Justin had to hold back a whoop of joy. He forced himself to shrug, adopting an indifferent expression. 'I guess I can cope with sitting out the next half . . . if you *really* think it's a good idea.'

Silently, he willed his legs: *Come on! We can do this! Just one last play, then freedom!*

Unfortunately, his legs didn't seem to be paying any attention to his bribery. Stabbing pain shot up them as he took his position for the play.

Justin gritted his teeth. *I will do whatever it takes to sit out the next half!*

As he got ready, Mackenzie started up a new cheer: 'We know we'll win – 'cos we've got Just*in*!'

186

As long as I can do this, he answered silently, *I don't care what you cheer.*

His eyes narrowed as he waited for Kyle's signal. *And . . . go!*

Kyle caught the ball, and Justin barrelled towards the defensive line. Growling as fiercely as a wolf, he forced his way through the line of players, shoving a space clear for himself. *No one can stop me!*

With a grunt of effort, he broke through and forced his legs to move faster, ignoring every bolt of pain they sent through him. He *had* to get downfield in time! As he raced across the AstroTurf, he heard the gasp of the crowd.

He knew what that meant . . .

Kyle had hefted the ball downfield. Justin *had* to get there in time to catch it!

The shadow of the ball passed over him . . . going much, much too fast.

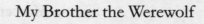

I'm not going to make it, he realised.

It didn't matter how hard he pushed himself: his wrung-out legs just wouldn't move fast enough. There was nothing he could do.

Unless . . .

It was a gamble. He'd never tried it in practice. But maybe, just maybe . . .

He thought of Riley forcing herself onward with no sleep. He thought of Daniel winning the battle of the bands, despite having his song stolen.

With a roar of effort, Justin launched himself into the air, jumping as high as he could.

The tips of his fingers brushed against the ball . . .

. . . And his hands closed around it as he landed back on the ground at the opposition's twenty-yard line.

His feet hit the ground hard, just at the wrong angle. Losing his balance, Justin started to tip forward. He caught himself just in time, firming his grip around the ball. With a triumphant yell, he gathered himself up – and charged all the way into the end zone!

'Touchdown, Pine Wood!' the announcer boomed through the megaphone.

'*Woooooooooooooo!*'

'PACKER!'

'Way to go, man!'

The Beasts thundered down the field to surround him, roaring their approval as they pounded on his shoulders and his back. Buoyed up by adrenaline, Justin didn't even stagger under the onslaught.

'Way to fake human-ness!' Ed whispered approvingly, as he gave Justin a stinging high-five. 'That was great acting!'

'Heh.' Justin grinned. 'Thanks, um, *dawg*. It was nothing.'

'No?' Kyle raised his eyebrows, his gaze intent. 'Don't sell yourself short, Packer.' He reached out to grab Justin's hand for a shake. 'Trust me. We want to know what you're *really* made of.'

His hand gripped Justin's and squeezed it – *hard*.

Justin froze as he saw Kyle's eyes narrow in calculation. That extra-hard hand-squeeze wasn't just enthusiasm or carelessness, was it? No, it was a *test* – a test of how strong Justin really was . . . whether he would feel pain . . .

. . . whether he *really* was a werewolf!

Justin gave Kyle a big grin and squeezed back with all his might. The TD buzz was so strong, he didn't even feel any pain where Kyle's hand crushed into his.

I made the Rabid Wolf play, after all, Justin thought as he smiled fiercely at the leader of the Beasts. *I made our twenty-point lead. And you can't even try to pretend that I don't belong here.*

The whistle blew for half-time. Kyle let go of Justin's hand with a shrug. As the home crowd cheered for Pine Wood, the whole group of Beasts made their way back to the sidelines, whooping and cheering right along with their fans.

Justin trailed slightly behind, searching the crowd in the stands. Riley had to be somewhere. If he could only spot her . . .

Oh, no. Someone else had spotted *him*! Mackenzie was standing on tiptoes among her cheerleaders. Her lips curved as he met her eye. She lifted one pom-pom to beckon him over.

Quickly, Justin dived into the middle of the Beasts to take cover. Even in the middle of them, though, he could feel Mackenzie glaring after him. He tried not to look back at her as he settled on a bench between his teammates.

The whole crowd quieted as Principal Caine strode on to the field, carrying two envelopes in one hand, and a microphone in the other.

Justin licked his lips nervously. Out of the corner of his eye, he could see Mackenzie going taut with excitement.

Here we go.

Those envelopes could only symbolise one thing right now: the naming of the Homecoming King and Queen.

'Hey, Packer, it's your moment.' Chris jostled him with one elbow, grinning. 'Did you vote for yourself?'

'Dude, you *know* he did,' Ed answered from Justin's other side. 'How else would he get to dance with Mackenzie in front of the whole school?'

Argh! Justin gripped the bench so tightly, his fingers hurt. If he had to dance with Mackenzie in front of the whole school tonight, then he'd be dancing with her in front of Riley! And what would Riley think of him then?

He couldn't be Homecoming King. He just couldn't.

'Now, students,' said Principal Caine, 'I'm sure . . .' she pursed her lips, '. . . we're all thrilled to finally share this moment.'

She sounded as depressed as if she were at a funeral. *I just might be*, Justin thought.

'Our Homecoming King for this year is . . .' Principal Caine opened the envelope.

Please don't let it be Mackenzie, Justin thought. *Well, no — it can be Mackenzie, as long as it's not Mackenzie and* me! *Please not me . . . Please not me . . .*

Principal Caine sighed into the microphone. 'Justin Packer!'

Seriously? Justin's mouth dropped open. He'd expected to feel embarrassed . . . but actually, it felt really good. All those people had voted for him.

'Come on, man!' Ed pulled him to his feet. 'Take a bow!'

'Um . . .' Nervously, Justin pulled himself up and bobbed his head in a bow. The applause from the stands got even louder. Despite himself, he felt his smile become a real one.

He desperately did *not* want to be King to Mackenzie's Queen. But he had to admit . . . it was nice to be liked.

As Mackenzie beamed at him triumphantly, Justin stood on tiptoes, trying to search out Riley's face in the crowd. He couldn't see her anywhere.

'And now . . .' Principal Caine cleared her throat. The field fell silent.

Justin held himself poised on his aching legs, waiting for the final judgment. *This is it!*

'We can hardly have a King without a Queen,' said Principal Caine dryly, 'and therefore, the student chosen as Pine Wood's Homecoming Queen is . . .'

Is . . .? Justin couldn't breathe.

Principal Caine gave a small, tight smile. '. . . going to be announced at the Dance itself!' She slipped the second envelope into her pocket. 'Enjoy the second half of the game, everyone.'

All the strength in Justin's legs gave out in a whoosh. He flopped on to the bench with a groan.

'Geez, Packer.' Kyle shook his head. 'You're taking this all pretty seriously. I didn't think you cared that much about popularity. Are you that worried you might not get to dance with your girlfriend?'

'Mackenzie is *not* my girlfriend,' Justin mumbled. He closed his eyes, feeling pain arc up and down the muscles of his legs.

195

'She sure cheers like she's your girlfriend,' Chris said.

Ed snorted. 'She sure *looks* at you like she's your girlfriend.'

'Maybe she'll only be his girlfriend if she wins,' Kyle said. 'That would explain why he's so nervous.'

'Whatever.' Justin gritted his teeth, but he didn't say any more, even when they kept on teasing him. He was too tense to argue about it. If he did, he might just explode from pressure and give everything away.

Why hadn't Principal Caine just gone ahead and announced the Homecoming Queen when everyone was expecting her to, to put them all out of their misery?

Please let it be Debi, not Mackenzie. Please let Riley's campaigning have worked!

At that, he felt his first small burst of relief.

What am I thinking? This is Riley. Of course it worked!

Riley was brilliant at everything she did. She was the Queen of Organisation! With Riley in charge of Debi's campaign, it was sure to win . . . and that meant that there was *no* possibility of Justin having to dance with Mackenzie tonight, in front of Riley.

Justin sagged with relief at the realisation. Finally relaxing, he waved his teammates off as they took their places on the field for the second half. Stretching out his aching legs, he prepared to enjoy the rest of the game.

Then he accidentally caught Mackenzie's gaze. She was grinning straight at him. Across the field, she pointed first at Justin, then at herself. '*You and me*,' she mouthed. '*Tonight.*'

Then she reached up to set an invisible crown on her head.

Justin groaned. All of his certainty drained away, replaced by sheer desperation.

Please let Riley's campaign have worked!

Chapter Ten

Daniel had been in his school gym more times than he could count, but it had never felt so big before – or so stomach-clenchingly intimidating.

This is getting way too real.

Sure, there were cheerful ribbons and banners hung all around the gym, and tables full of delicious food set out for the dance, all set up by Riley – but Daniel didn't care about any of those. All he cared about was the makeshift wooden stage raised above the floor on the far end of the gym. Otto's drum kit was already set up at the back, and the microphone and amplifiers were plugged in, just waiting for the band to hop on once the dancers arrived.

It looked real. It looked *professional*. No matter how many students flooded in to pack the gym once the Dance started, every single one of them would be able to see and hear *In Sheep's Clothing*.

Daniel was suddenly feeling sick! Worse than sick, he was feeling like he might *turn*.

Pushing one hand hard over his stomach, he bent over his guitar so that no one could see his face. He was standing in the shadow of the stage. To anyone who looked across the gym, he hoped he'd just look like he was taking his warm-up duties seriously.

Just calm down, he told himself, as he had done when the change had come over him after he argued with Milo. *Just calm down and you won't change . . . This is perfectly normal. You're just an ordinary thirteen-year-old boy with an ace band who is getting ready for his . . .*

He swallowed hard, as nausea almost overwhelmed him . . . *Gig!*

Somehow, the single word that he most loved saying and thinking had suddenly become the most terrifying syllable in the entire English language.

This is a big mistake.

His fingers froze on his guitar strings. His mouth went dry as his pulse started pounding in his ears.

What had he been thinking, auditioning the band for a real gig? They weren't ready! They needed more practice! Maybe he should go tell that to Principal Caine right now. They might be ready in another month . . . or maybe three months would be better . . . or should he give them a whole year just to be on the safe side?

I have to call this off!

Steeling himself, he looked up. Nathan and Otto were grinning and bantering with each other as they chowed down on nacho dip from one of the side tables covered with food. *They* didn't look nervous. Why weren't they nervous?

Daniel groaned silently. Maybe he really was the only one with something to fear. OK, he admitted it: he had a *lot* to fear.

What if he flubbed a note with the whole school listening? What if his wolf nails snapped every string on his guitar? What if . . . He closed his eyes in pain as he realised the worst possibility of all: *What if everybody laughs at my lyrics?*

'Hey, Daniel! Getting excited?'

His eyes flew open. Debi was walking straight towards him across the gym, wearing a sleek purple dress that swished around her legs. Her vibrant red hair fell loose around her shoulders, and long purple gloves stretched to her elbows. She looked as if she could have stepped straight out of the pages of one of his favourite comic books!

'Wow.' Daniel blinked. 'You look . . .' *Wait. Stop!* His words screeched to a halt as his brain caught up with him. *Do NOT tell the girl you like that she looks like a comic book superhero! She'll think you're a geek!*

'Do I look OK?' Grinning, she twirled around to show off the dress. 'What do you think – is it acceptable at Pine Wood to come to the Homecoming Dance dressed like you're going to fight crime?'

She really is the perfect girl!

'Absolutely,' Daniel said. 'If you need a sidekick, I'm there!'

'Oh, yeah?' She raised one eyebrow, looking him up and down. 'Superheroes have to be pretty careful when they're choosing their sidekicks, you know. What would *your* special skills be?'

'Uh . . .' Daniel choked. *She really does not want to know the honest answer to that question!* 'How about . . . I'll hypnotise villains with my music?'

'Hmm.' Debi's eyebrows scrunched together adorably. Then she smiled and winked at him. 'OK. I don't know about you, but *Daring Debi and the Hypno-Kid* is definitely a comic *I* would read!'

'Me, too,' Daniel agreed. His voice came out sounding breathless. He barely noticed his own feet moving, carrying him closer to her. As subtly as he could, he glanced down at his hands. *Phew. No wolfiness yet!* He was actually *comfortable* around this girl. 'Maybe —'

'Hey, guys! I'm here!' Riley rushed towards them. For once, she wasn't carrying any clipboards, but the shadows under her eyes were almost as dark as her band T-shirt. 'Sorry I'm running late! I just had to do the last bits of set-up first. My voice is all warmed up and ready to go, though. I promise!'

'It all looks great, Riley,' Debi said. She gestured to the tables of food and drink at the side of the room, and the massive banners hanging from the ceiling.

'Debi's right.' Now that he was feeling a little more relaxed, Daniel looked around the gym with a new perspective. 'You've worked really hard, and it looks fantastic. Oh, and that nacho dip is the best I've ever tasted.' He gestured at Nathan and Otto. 'They haven't been able to stop eating it since we got here! Where did you find it?'

'Oh, that? It's homemade.' Riley frowned, peering towards the table where Nathan and Otto had settled. 'Do you think there's enough? I made eight tubs, but —'

'Wait a minute.' Daniel stared at her. 'Are you telling us you made the food *yourself*? At the same time as organising absolutely everything?'

Riley shrugged, looking uncomfortable. 'I had some time last night.'

'*When?*' Daniel shook his head in disbelief.

She frowned. 'Um . . . I think it was right after midnight, maybe? I was getting pretty tired, so I needed to do something on my feet for a while before I went back to working on the banners.'

Debi frowned at her. 'Have you gotten *any* sleep this week, Riley?'

'Well . . .'

As Riley shook her head, Daniel felt his stomach sink, and all his earlier nerves return. The big doors at the end of the gym had just been propped open, and students were flooding in, dressed up like movie stars. They were all chattering and laughing with excitement. Within moments, the whole gym would be packed with people. *In Sheep's Clothing* was about to perform their first real gig in just five minutes, in front of the entire school . . . and their lead singer looked as if she could topple over at any moment!

This is going to be even more of a disaster than I realised!

Then Daniel met Riley's gaze and saw the stubbornness deep within it like a flame. Her shoulders squared, and Daniel relaxed.

How could I forget? This isn't just anyone we're talking about. This is Riley Carter.

He'd known Riley since kindergarten, and she had never, *ever* given up on anything important. She had brought it all for the audition, despite how exhausted she had been then, and she'd bring it now, too, because they needed it.

. . . and if she could do it . . . then Daniel could, too.

'Looks like show time,' Debi said. She squeezed Daniel's arm. 'Good luck!'

Principal Caine strode up the steps to the stage, wearing her usual grey suit and looking grimmer than ever. The doors to the gym closed behind the final students – the football team, arriving in a pack – as she stepped up to the microphone, clearing her throat.

'Ahem.' She cleared her throat again, even as the gym fell silent. 'Ahem.' Now everyone was watching and waiting. 'Ahem!'

Get on with it! Daniel thought. His muscles were tight, but now it was with anticipation, not fear. *I want to rock!*

Principal Caine smiled thinly as she looked around the crowded gym. 'Welcome, everyone, to this year's Homecoming Dance,' she said. 'And now it is my honour to announce this year's Homecoming Queen as . . .'

She slipped the envelope out of her pocket.

This is it. Daniel saw Riley grab Debi's hand

supportively, standing in solidarity with her candidate.

Daniel aimed a smile at Debi. She'd never seemed to care about the results of this competition, but who knew how she really felt?

He caught sight of Justin's anguished face across the crowd. *There's one person who really cares!*

On the other side of the gym, Mackenzie Barton was smiling smugly, dressed in a floor-length pink poofy dress and surrounded by followers who looked like they were already busy congratulating her. Daniel gritted his teeth.

He only realised he was scowling when he caught Debi's startled gaze. *Uh-oh.* He tried to adjust his expression, but it was too late. She had already turned back to face Principal Caine, wincing as Riley's hand visibly tightened.

She'll win, Daniel reassured himself. *She has to win, for Justin's sake.*

But if she does . . . He sighed. Would a Homecoming Queen like Debi ever really be interested in a scruffy rock band frontman and secret werewolf like him?

Principal Caine opened the envelope and withdrew a slip of paper. The whole gym seemed to freeze in anticipation.

'. . . Riley Carter!' she read. 'Riley Carter is our Homecoming Queen.'

There was a moment of stunned silence. Then a voice rang out:

'WHAT?!'

Mackenzie Barton had turned bright red with fury.

'Uhm . . . Yeah . . .' Riley said, looking like she's been shaken away from a dream. '*What?!*'

'How is it even possible?' Mackenzie bellowed.

Principal Caine aimed a stern look at Mackenzie through her glasses. 'The votes were tallied, young lady, and Miss Carter won. In fact, almost all of the votes were for her.'

'But . . .' Riley shook her head, still holding Debi's hand and looking stunned. 'I don't understand. I didn't even know that I'd been nominated!'

Principal Caine sighed. 'And *that* is because you were too busy talking about *organising* the Homecoming, rather than listening to see if you were a part of it!'

'But I . . . I . . .' Riley looked as if she might faint.

'This is outrageous!' Mackenzie spun around, scowling. 'I refuse to take part in this scandal!'

She stomped out of the gym, her high heels clicking against the floor, and slammed the doors behind her with a crash. The sound was exactly what Daniel had needed to push him into action.

Riley had been his friend since kindergarten.

He needed to support her.

Justin must have started moving even earlier. He pushed his way to Riley through the crowded gym even before Daniel got to her . . . but she didn't seem to notice either of them. All of her attention was on Debi.

'I'm so sorry!' she wailed. 'I had no idea, Debi – I promise, I would *never* have competed against you, not when I was your campaign manager! If I'd only realised –'

'Don't worry, Riley!' Laughing, Debi hugged her. 'Guess what? I voted for you, too! You absolutely *deserved* to win. Clearly, this whole school appreciates how much effort you go to, to make sure that we all have fun!'

'That's right,' Justin chimed in, beaming with pride. 'We *love* that about you.'

At his words, Riley went still, her eyes widening in surprise. Her face flushed pink.

Debi looked between Justin and Riley with her lips twitching. As Daniel watched, a wave of red swept across his brother's face as Justin seemed to finally realise what he had just said. 'We *all* love that about you,' Justin added quickly.

Oops. Grinning, Daniel stepped in to cover for his mortified twin. 'No one does more for this school than you do, Riley. And it's a great day when *that* gets the popular vote, instead of the self-appointed Queen Bee.'

'Absolutely.' Debi smiled approvingly at Daniel. 'I can't think of anyone I'd rather have as Queen for the next week!'

'But I can't!' Riley shook her head frantically. 'You guys don't understand. I'm not a queen! I'm an *organiser*, not a leader!'

'Riley . . .' Daniel sighed. 'Who could possibly be a better leader? You've *always* been the Queen of Organisation. Now you're the Homecoming

Queen, too! It just makes sense.'

'*Perfect* sense,' Debi agreed, and gave Riley another tight hug. 'And you're going to be great. I promise.'

'Ahem!' Principal Caine cleared her throat loudly from the stage just by them. 'I hesitate to interrupt this . . . ahem . . . "touching" moment . . . but have you forgotten something, Mr Packer?'

'Sorry?' Daniel frowned up at her. 'What did I forget?'

Principal Caine rolled her eyes. 'You are *supposed* to be on stage right now with your band. You're playing the song that the King and Queen dance to!'

Oh, no. Daniel saw the horrified realisation bloom in Riley's expression – they were figuring out their biggest problem at the same time.

Nathan had come up next to him. 'But how

are we supposed to perform with our lead singer on the dance floor?'

'Uh . . .' Daniel swallowed hard, fighting down panic. 'Let me just take a minute to figure out how to do that.'

'If you must.' Muttering to herself, Principal Caine walked down the steps. She was speaking too softly for anyone else to hear, but Daniel's werewolf hearing picked up her words perfectly: 'As if it would make a difference who sang those depressing, too-loud songs anyway!'

Ouch. He winced.

Riley obviously took his expression the wrong way. 'I'm so sorry, Daniel. I had no idea. But I *can't* sing and dance at the same time! I'd just drop the microphone – and then trip over it!'

Daniel snorted at the image, his shoulders relaxing. 'Don't worry about it.' Principal Caine's words had sparked off an idea in the back of his mind. She thought their songs were all depressing, huh? Well, he'd show her just how wrong she was – and give his brother a slow dance to remember.

'You just take your place on the dance floor and don't worry about anything else,' he told Riley. 'I have an idea . . .'

Maybe he should have felt more nervous. But with Riley appointed Queen – and Debi revealed as a secret comic book fan! – suddenly everything seemed possible.

A few minutes later, Riley and Justin were in place in the centre of the gym, while Daniel and his other band mates stood huddled on the stage. 'Don't worry,' he whispered to them. 'You *will* be able to play the song. Just watch me for the key-changes and try to keep up . . .'

Putting on a confident smile, he strode to the front of the stage, while Otto and Nathan took their places behind him. The rest of the school was gathered in a half-circle around the gym, making plenty of room for the King and Queen's first dance. As Daniel stepped up to the microphone, he could feel the tangible tension and anticipation of the crowd hanging thick in the air, making his skin prickle.

Daniel was relieved that he was wearing long sleeves, as he felt wolf hair prickling and growing on his arms.

It doesn't matter. I can do this!

'Hey, Pine Wood!' he roared into the microphone. 'We've got a new song just for you guys, tonight, and our very own Homecoming King and Queen are going to dance to it.'

The crowd roared back, 'Go Pine Wood!' with happy applause, and Daniel took a deep breath. *Here goes!*

With a rock-star howl, he jumped into the air and hit the opening chord of *No More Puppy Love*.

Otto's drums kicked in behind him, strong and certain, while Nathan soon picked up the rhythm for his guitar. As Daniel played the opening riff, he saw heads all around the crowded gym start to nod in time with the music. Even Principal Caine seemed to be sneering a little less than usual!

'. . . *Red like fire, my heart's desire . . .*'

It was the moment of truth. Daniel forced himself to glance down to where Debi stood by the stage.

He found her grinning up at him in pure delight.

From the look in her eyes, she knew exactly who this song had been written about – and she didn't mind one bit!

What was I so afraid of this whole time?

As exhilaration flooded him, Daniel sung the rest of the song straight at her. Even though Justin and Riley had the dance floor to themselves, the whole crowd was dancing in place now. When he got to the chorus, hundreds of voices lifted to sing along, sending a thrill racing down his spine.

No one was laughing. He hadn't missed a single note. *No More Puppy Love* did not suck, after all . . . and as Debi beamed up at him he realised that he didn't either.

Daniel *rocked*!

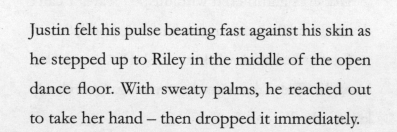

Justin felt his pulse beating fast against his skin as he stepped up to Riley in the middle of the open dance floor. With sweaty palms, he reached out to take her hand – then dropped it immediately.

Was I squeezing too hard? I can't even tell! Danger, danger! He swallowed hard, trying to control his panic. *I can't believe I get to dance with Riley. I cannot mess this up!*

Up onstage, his brother began to sing. The

sound hit Justin like a ball on the football field. He and Riley should be dancing right now, not just *staring* at each other.

Come on, cub! You can do this! Make the play!

'Justin?' Riley's whisper sounded almost as panicked as he felt.

Immediately, concern took over. 'What's wrong?' Justin stepped closer, leaning in to keep their conversation private.

Her eyes glimmered with unshed tears. 'I can't do this! I can't dance in front of everybody!'

Justin frowned. 'Riley . . .' He shook his head, baffled. 'You can do anything. Everybody knows that!'

She looked down, biting her lip. 'Just look at me! I dressed to perform with the band, not to be a Homecoming Queen.'

'So?' Justin looked from her shining blonde hair, which was ornamented by a sparkling black fascinator, to her tight black band T-shirt and her sleek black trousers. 'You look great to me,' he said. 'And almost everyone in this gym voted for you, remember? That means they all think you're pretty cool, too.'

'But . . .' Riley closed her eyes for a moment, taking a deep breath. Then she looked directly at him with obvious pain in her eyes. 'Justin, haven't you ever noticed the fact that I'm a little bit . . . *clumsy?*'

That did it. The last of Justin's panic disappeared, swept away by a wave of protective pride.

'Riley,' he said, 'I have never thought that about you. And you are going to dance just fine.'

When he reached for her hand this time, his palms didn't sweat. He closed his fingers around hers like a promise.

Ever since he'd first met her all those years ago, Riley had always been so confident and in control. Now, though, she finally needed someone else's help. And Justin was *not* going to let her down.

Maybe he hadn't ever danced with a girl before, but he'd seen movies and TV shows. He knew how it was supposed to go. He stepped in closer, arranging their arms in the way he'd always seen dancing couples fit together. He felt her breath catch as he put his hand on her back. His heartbeat quickened as she laid her own hand on his shoulder.

This is Riley. I'm really dancing with Riley!

He'd never been so glad of all the footwork that he'd learned from playing football. He moved them back and forth in a slow, dreamy circle, guiding Riley in time with the ballad his brother was singing on stage. At first, Riley held herself stiffly, obviously afraid of making a mistake, or falling over. Then she met his eyes and smiled, and he felt her relax in his arms, leaning into him.

'*Thank you,*' she mouthed.

Justin shook his head, smiling back at her. 'Nothing to thank me for,' he whispered. 'I'm happy.'

We're dancing, he thought, knowing he was grinning goofily and not caring one bit. *And no one can call this NOT-a-date!*

However goofy his grin was, he knew it became the *officially* Stupidest Grin Ever as Riley *— can this really be happening? —* laid her head on his shoulder.

His twin's music swept through the gym, and Justin felt as if he'd been swept right along with it into a dream. And it had to be a dream. Real life was *never* this good!

Even as he thought that, he noticed a shift in Riley's movements. He wasn't just guiding her steps any more – he was moving her still body. In fact . . .

He choked on a silent laugh as he looked down at her peaceful face, her eyes closed.

I guess Riley really is dreaming now!

It was no wonder she'd *finally* fallen asleep. This was probably the first time she'd relaxed this whole week.

Come to think of it, now that all his own nerves had gone, Justin's own legs were seriously starting to ache from all that faking-werewolfness that he'd been doing lately – not to mention his big play in the Homecoming Game. He could quite happily take a nap of his own.

In the meantime, though, this felt amazingly good. Maybe he'd just lean on Riley for a second . . . and it couldn't hurt to close his own eyes, just for just a moment . . . he'd just rest his face in her soft hair . . . for a minute . . .

Daniel had never expected to break out laughing at his first real gig. But as he looked down at the couple in the centre of the dance floor, he had to fight not to crack up in the middle of his own love song.

No one else seemed to have noticed that Justin and Riley were doing anything different from a *very* slow slow-dance . . . but Daniel's hearing was wolf-sharp and couldn't be fooled. From their rhythmic breathing, it was obvious that both of them had fallen fast asleep. In fact, they would have both fallen over . . . were it not for each other.

Daniel grinned. Maybe he could use *that* line in a song!

Right now, though, it was time to finish up *No More Puppy Love* with his own very special addition: flat-out wolfish howling at the final chorus! He tipped back and let himself loose. As the howls rocked through him, wild and free, a feeling of *rightness* filled him, just like it had at that first werewolf gathering.

OK, so maybe he'd never planned on being a werewolf. Maybe he wasn't even anyone's idea of what a werewolf 'should' be. But as the howls ripped through his chest, Daniel knew one thing for sure: he was exactly *who* he had always been meant to be . . . no matter what anyone else might think about it.

He opened his eyes at the end of the song and found Kyle from the football team giving him a narrow-eyed, suspicious look from the gym floor. He thought he heard the quarterback mumbling beneath the wild applause that seemed to rattle the gym:

'Very realistic howling, Packer . . . *Daniel* Packer.'

Daniel kept a goofy grin on his face, pretending that he had not heard what Kyle had said. It took all his focus not to look in his direction – if he did, he knew that Kyle would know Daniel had heard . . .

And then Kyle would know the truth!

Just act normal, Daniel told himself. *Whatever 'normal' is in Pine Wood.*

He bowed to the crowd, still applauding. In the centre of the dance floor, Riley jolted awake, obviously woken by the noise. Daniel heard her gasp as she jerked upright, desperately trying to pat herself back into her normal neat-and-tidy self. Unfortunately, she only succeeded in messing up the fascinator clipped to her hair, so it hung off her head at a bizarre angle, making her hair look lopsided. Daniel choked back a laugh at the sight.

It sure didn't seem to bother Justin, though.

As soon as he woke up and saw her, his grin was as goofy as Daniel knew his own had been. It was tough to tell which twin was more elated at that moment. Daniel thought he would edge it when he heard Kyle talking to his friends about their next game. He seemed to have forgotten whatever suspicions he had had.

Daniel's first real gig had been a success . . . and so had his new song. As Debi smiled up at him from the crowd, wearing her superhero dress and gloves, Daniel realised something else, too: maybe it was time for him to take more risks.

Maybe it was time to take the biggest risk.

Maybe it's time to stop hiding the truth from her.

If Debi could accept him being a scruffy, hardcore rocker . . . maybe she would accept him being a werewolf, too.

She was so cool that he was finally ready to believe she just might.

Pine Wood Post Online Feature

Mackenzie's Musings
Bringing you all the IMPORTANT news from Pine Wood Junior High

Hi! Welcome to the latest edition of *Mackenzie's Musings*, with ME – Mackenzie Barton.

This week, it's our Homecoming Dance Edition and I just have to begin by saying how FINE I am with not being voted Homecoming Queen. Absolutely fine. You are probably already aware that, in a completely insane turn of events, Riley Carter NARROWLY WON . . . despite the fact that she DIDN'T EVEN KNOW SHE WAS NOMINATED. (Oops! Left the Caps Lock on. Oh well!)

Sadly for 'Her Majesty', the dance itself wasn't exactly legendary. One can't help wondering whether 'our' Queen would have been better off singing with her band, than on the dance floor. Not that *In Sheep's Clothing* were TOTALLY bad, or anything – just that I'm not sure all that *howling* was quite the right choice for a dance that needed more pink and less black.

And speaking of colour coordination, let me tell you all what's *hot* and what's *totally not*:

* Purple with orange is in: They totally go together. Black on black is out: It's not matching, it's just lazy!

* Fascinators: in. Corsages: out. (More plumage, less jungle chic.)

* Strappy sandals: in. Killer heels: out. (More dancing, less falling over – unless you're Riley Carter, who could fall over when she's lying down!)

Now that's out of the way, what else do I

want to talk about? Well, there's the dress that I wore for the dance itself. A purple gown with a gorgeous orange wrap. My fascinator was worn at the side so that if I were to be given a crown, for any reason, my amazing up-do wouldn't be disturbed. It would have been perfect for a Queen. Not that I'm complaining, of course, but I love-love-LOVED my outfit. I might even wear it a SECOND TIME.

Final Mackenzie Musing – I have, AT LAST, got my Blu-ray copy of *The Groves*, starring my favourite actor, Jackson Caulfield. I LOVE this movie – so funny and so sweet. And I seriously think people need to calm down on the Jessica Phelps hate – yes, she said mean things at the Bright Star Awards earlier this year, but sometimes it's brave to speak your mind. My fellow cheerleaders often say I'm VERY brave.

Anyway – if you haven't seen *The*

Groves, you need to IMPROVE YOUR LIFE immediately and check it out.

It's time for me to stop, but I would NEVER be cruel enough to let you go without the next eagerly awaited instalment of . . .

Mackenzie's Murmurs!

Where I, Mackenzie Barton, shine my 'Torch of Truth' on the secrets my peers would rather keep hidden . . .

This Week's Whispers:

* One Pine Wood 9th grader seriously needs a haircut. You know who you are.

* We expect there to be love in the air at a Homecoming Dance, but it wasn't just the students getting mushy. Numerous reports have come in of two teachers making eyes at each other across the dancefloor. Be careful, Ms XX and Mr XX – you're not the romantic ninjas you think you are!

* Halloween is just a few weeks away. What's the betting that half of the football team will go as werewolves . . . *again*? Sigh. They should take a leaf out of my book and change it up a bit. Last year I went as a fairy, and so did my cheer squad. The year before it was princesses. The year before that it was fairy princesses. Have some imagination, guys!

COMMENTS ON THIS FEATURE:

DANIEL PACKER says: Mackenzie, I like my hair just fine, thank you.

'RIGHTEOUS' MILO says: Are you crazy? That band SUCKED. Who wants to hear love songs at a dance? It was a SCANDAL that they were chosen. A travesty.